The Short Story: A Very Short Introduction

VERY SHORT INTRODUCTIONS are for anyone wanting a stimulating and accessible way into a new subject. They are written by experts, and have been translated into more than 45 different languages.

The series began in 1995, and now covers a wide variety of topics in every discipline. The VSI library currently contains over 650 volumes—a Very Short Introduction to everything from Psychology and Philosophy of Science to American History and Relativity—and continues to grow in every subject area.

Very Short Introductions available now:

ABOLITIONISM Richard S. Newman
THE ABRAHAMIC RELIGIONS Charles L. Cohen
ACCOUNTING Christopher Nobes
ADOLESCENCE Peter K. Smith
ADVERTISING Winston Fletcher
AERIAL WARFARE Frank Ledwidge
AESTHETICS Bence Nanay
AFRICAN AMERICAN RELIGION Eddie S. Glaude Jr
AFRICAN HISTORY John Parker and Richard Rathbone
AFRICAN POLITICS Ian Taylor
AFRICAN RELIGIONS Jacob K. Olupona
AGEING Nancy A. Pachana
AGNOSTICISM Robin Le Poidevin
AGRICULTURE Paul Brassley and Richard Soffe
ALEXANDER THE GREAT Hugh Bowden
ALGEBRA Peter M. Higgins
AMERICAN BUSINESS HISTORY Walter A. Friedman
AMERICAN CULTURAL HISTORY Eric Avila
AMERICAN FOREIGN RELATIONS Andrew Preston
AMERICAN HISTORY Paul S. Boyer
AMERICAN IMMIGRATION David A. Gerber
AMERICAN INTELLECTUAL HISTORY Jennifer Ratner-Rosenhagen
AMERICAN LEGAL HISTORY G. Edward White
AMERICAN MILITARY HISTORY Joseph T. Glatthaar
AMERICAN NAVAL HISTORY Craig L. Symonds
AMERICAN POLITICAL HISTORY Donald Critchlow
AMERICAN POLITICAL PARTIES AND ELECTIONS L. Sandy Maisel
AMERICAN POLITICS Richard M. Valelly
THE AMERICAN PRESIDENCY Charles O. Jones
THE AMERICAN REVOLUTION Robert J. Allison
AMERICAN SLAVERY Heather Andrea Williams
THE AMERICAN SOUTH Charles Reagan Wilson
THE AMERICAN WEST Stephen Aron
AMERICAN WOMEN'S HISTORY Susan Ware
AMPHIBIANS T. S. Kemp
ANAESTHESIA Aidan O'Donnell
ANALYTIC PHILOSOPHY Michael Beaney
ANARCHISM Colin Ward
ANCIENT ASSYRIA Karen Radner
ANCIENT EGYPT Ian Shaw
ANCIENT EGYPTIAN ART AND ARCHITECTURE Christina Riggs
ANCIENT GREECE Paul Cartledge

THE ANCIENT NEAR EAST Amanda H. Podany
ANCIENT PHILOSOPHY Julia Annas
ANCIENT WARFARE Harry Sidebottom
ANGELS David Albert Jones
ANGLICANISM Mark Chapman
THE ANGLO-SAXON AGE John Blair
ANIMAL BEHAVIOUR Tristram D. Wyatt
THE ANIMAL KINGDOM Peter Holland
ANIMAL RIGHTS David DeGrazia
THE ANTARCTIC Klaus Dodds
ANTHROPOCENE Erle C. Ellis
ANTISEMITISM Steven Beller
ANXIETY Daniel Freeman and Jason Freeman
THE APOCRYPHAL GOSPELS Paul Foster
APPLIED MATHEMATICS Alain Goriely
THOMAS AQUINAS Fergus Kerr
ARBITRATION Thomas Schultz and Thomas Grant
ARCHAEOLOGY Paul Bahn
ARCHITECTURE Andrew Ballantyne
THE ARCTIC Klaus Dodds and Jamie Woodward
ARISTOCRACY William Doyle
ARISTOTLE Jonathan Barnes
ART HISTORY Dana Arnold
ART THEORY Cynthia Freeland
ARTIFICIAL INTELLIGENCE Margaret A. Boden
ASIAN AMERICAN HISTORY Madeline Y. Hsu
ASTROBIOLOGY David C. Catling
ASTROPHYSICS James Binney
ATHEISM Julian Baggini
THE ATMOSPHERE Paul I. Palmer
AUGUSTINE Henry Chadwick
AUSTRALIA Kenneth Morgan
AUTISM Uta Frith
AUTOBIOGRAPHY Laura Marcus
THE AVANT GARDE David Cottington
THE AZTECS Davíd Carrasco
BABYLONIA Trevor Bryce
BACTERIA Sebastian G. B. Amyes
BANKING John Goddard and John O. S. Wilson
BARTHES Jonathan Culler
THE BEATS David Sterritt
BEAUTY Roger Scruton
BEHAVIOURAL ECONOMICS Michelle Baddeley
BESTSELLERS John Sutherland
THE BIBLE John Riches
BIBLICAL ARCHAEOLOGY Eric H. Cline
BIG DATA Dawn E. Holmes
BIOCHEMISTRY Mark Lorch
BIOGEOGRAPHY Mark V. Lomolino
BIOGRAPHY Hermione Lee
BIOMETRICS Michael Fairhurst
BLACK HOLES Katherine Blundell
BLASPHEMY Yvonne Sherwood
BLOOD Chris Cooper
THE BLUES Elijah Wald
THE BODY Chris Shilling
THE BOOK OF COMMON PRAYER Brian Cummings
THE BOOK OF MORMON Terryl Givens
BORDERS Alexander C. Diener and Joshua Hagen
THE BRAIN Michael O'Shea
BRANDING Robert Jones
THE BRICS Andrew F. Cooper
THE BRITISH CONSTITUTION Martin Loughlin
THE BRITISH EMPIRE Ashley Jackson
BRITISH POLITICS Tony Wright
BUDDHA Michael Carrithers
BUDDHISM Damien Keown
BUDDHIST ETHICS Damien Keown
BYZANTIUM Peter Sarris
CALVINISM Jon Balserak
ALBERT CAMUS Oliver Gloag
CANADA Donald Wright
CANCER Nicholas James
CAPITALISM James Fulcher
CATHOLICISM Gerald O'Collins
CAUSATION Stephen Mumford and Rani Lill Anjum
THE CELL Terence Allen and Graham Cowling
THE CELTS Barry Cunliffe
CHAOS Leonard Smith

GEOFFREY CHAUCER David Wallace
CHEMISTRY Peter Atkins
CHILD PSYCHOLOGY Usha Goswami
CHILDREN'S LITERATURE Kimberley Reynolds
CHINESE LITERATURE Sabina Knight
CHOICE THEORY Michael Allingham
CHRISTIAN ART Beth Williamson
CHRISTIAN ETHICS D. Stephen Long
CHRISTIANITY Linda Woodhead
CIRCADIAN RHYTHMS Russell Foster and Leon Kreitzman
CITIZENSHIP Richard Bellamy
CITY PLANNING Carl Abbott
CIVIL ENGINEERING David Muir Wood
CLASSICAL LITERATURE William Allan
CLASSICAL MYTHOLOGY Helen Morales
CLASSICS Mary Beard and John Henderson
CLAUSEWITZ Michael Howard
CLIMATE Mark Maslin
CLIMATE CHANGE Mark Maslin
CLINICAL PSYCHOLOGY Susan Llewelyn and Katie Aafjes-van Doorn
COGNITIVE NEUROSCIENCE Richard Passingham
THE COLD WAR Robert J. McMahon
COLONIAL AMERICA Alan Taylor
COLONIAL LATIN AMERICAN LITERATURE Rolena Adorno
COMBINATORICS Robin Wilson
COMEDY Matthew Bevis
COMMUNISM Leslie Holmes
COMPARATIVE LITERATURE Ben Hutchinson
COMPETITION AND ANTITRUST LAW Ariel Ezrachi
COMPLEXITY John H. Holland
THE COMPUTER Darrel Ince
COMPUTER SCIENCE Subrata Dasgupta
CONCENTRATION CAMPS Dan Stone
CONFUCIANISM Daniel K. Gardner
THE CONQUISTADORS Matthew Restall and Felipe Fernández-Armesto
CONSCIENCE Paul Strohm
CONSCIOUSNESS Susan Blackmore
CONTEMPORARY ART Julian Stallabrass
CONTEMPORARY FICTION Robert Eaglestone
CONTINENTAL PHILOSOPHY Simon Critchley
COPERNICUS Owen Gingerich
CORAL REEFS Charles Sheppard
CORPORATE SOCIAL RESPONSIBILITY Jeremy Moon
CORRUPTION Leslie Holmes
COSMOLOGY Peter Coles
COUNTRY MUSIC Richard Carlin
CREATIVITY Vlad Glăveanu
CRIME FICTION Richard Bradford
CRIMINAL JUSTICE Julian V. Roberts
CRIMINOLOGY Tim Newburn
CRITICAL THEORY Stephen Eric Bronner
THE CRUSADES Christopher Tyerman
CRYPTOGRAPHY Fred Piper and Sean Murphy
CRYSTALLOGRAPHY A. M. Glazer
THE CULTURAL REVOLUTION Richard Curt Kraus
DADA AND SURREALISM David Hopkins
DANTE Peter Hainsworth and David Robey
DARWIN Jonathan Howard
THE DEAD SEA SCROLLS Timothy H. Lim
DECADENCE David Weir
DECOLONIZATION Dane Kennedy
DEMENTIA Kathleen Taylor
DEMOCRACY Bernard Crick
DEMOGRAPHY Sarah Harper
DEPRESSION Jan Scott and Mary Jane Tacchi
DERRIDA Simon Glendinning
DESCARTES Tom Sorell
DESERTS Nick Middleton
DESIGN John Heskett
DEVELOPMENT Ian Goldin
DEVELOPMENTAL BIOLOGY Lewis Wolpert
THE DEVIL Darren Oldridge
DIASPORA Kevin Kenny

CHARLES DICKENS Jenny Hartley
DICTIONARIES Lynda Mugglestone
DINOSAURS David Norman
DIPLOMATIC HISTORY Joseph M. Siracusa
DOCUMENTARY FILM Patricia Aufderheide
DREAMING J. Allan Hobson
DRUGS Les Iversen
DRUIDS Barry Cunliffe
DYNASTY Jeroen Duindam
DYSLEXIA Margaret J. Snowling
EARLY MUSIC Thomas Forrest Kelly
THE EARTH Martin Redfern
EARTH SYSTEM SCIENCE Tim Lenton
ECOLOGY Jaboury Ghazoul
ECONOMICS Partha Dasgupta
EDUCATION Gary Thomas
EGYPTIAN MYTH Geraldine Pinch
EIGHTEENTH-CENTURY BRITAIN Paul Langford
THE ELEMENTS Philip Ball
EMOTION Dylan Evans
EMPIRE Stephen Howe
ENERGY SYSTEMS Nick Jenkins
ENGELS Terrell Carver
ENGINEERING David Blockley
THE ENGLISH LANGUAGE Simon Horobin
ENGLISH LITERATURE Jonathan Bate
THE ENLIGHTENMENT John Robertson
ENTREPRENEURSHIP Paul Westhead and Mike Wright
ENVIRONMENTAL ECONOMICS Stephen Smith
ENVIRONMENTAL ETHICS Robin Attfield
ENVIRONMENTAL LAW Elizabeth Fisher
ENVIRONMENTAL POLITICS Andrew Dobson
ENZYMES Paul Engel
EPICUREANISM Catherine Wilson
EPIDEMIOLOGY Rodolfo Saracci
ETHICS Simon Blackburn
ETHNOMUSICOLOGY Timothy Rice
THE ETRUSCANS Christopher Smith
EUGENICS Philippa Levine
THE EUROPEAN UNION Simon Usherwood and John Pinder
EUROPEAN UNION LAW Anthony Arnull
EVOLUTION Brian and Deborah Charlesworth
EXISTENTIALISM Thomas Flynn
EXPLORATION Stewart A. Weaver
EXTINCTION Paul B. Wignall
THE EYE Michael Land
FAIRY TALE Marina Warner
FAMILY LAW Jonathan Herring
MICHAEL FARADAY Frank A. J. L. James
FASCISM Kevin Passmore
FASHION Rebecca Arnold
FEDERALISM Mark J. Rozell and Clyde Wilcox
FEMINISM Margaret Walters
FILM Michael Wood
FILM MUSIC Kathryn Kalinak
FILM NOIR James Naremore
FIRE Andrew C. Scott
THE FIRST WORLD WAR Michael Howard
FOLK MUSIC Mark Slobin
FOOD John Krebs
FORENSIC PSYCHOLOGY David Canter
FORENSIC SCIENCE Jim Fraser
FORESTS Jaboury Ghazoul
FOSSILS Keith Thomson
FOUCAULT Gary Gutting
THE FOUNDING FATHERS R. B. Bernstein
FRACTALS Kenneth Falconer
FREE SPEECH Nigel Warburton
FREE WILL Thomas Pink
FREEMASONRY Andreas Önnerfors
FRENCH LITERATURE John D. Lyons
FRENCH PHILOSOPHY Stephen Gaukroger and Knox Peden
THE FRENCH REVOLUTION William Doyle
FREUD Anthony Storr
FUNDAMENTALISM Malise Ruthven
FUNGI Nicholas P. Money
THE FUTURE Jennifer M. Gidley
GALAXIES John Gribbin
GALILEO Stillman Drake

GAME THEORY Ken Binmore
GANDHI Bhikhu Parekh
GARDEN HISTORY Gordon Campbell
GENES Jonathan Slack
GENIUS Andrew Robinson
GENOMICS John Archibald
GEOGRAPHY John Matthews and David Herbert
GEOLOGY Jan Zalasiewicz
GEOPHYSICS William Lowrie
GEOPOLITICS Klaus Dodds
GERMAN LITERATURE Nicholas Boyle
GERMAN PHILOSOPHY Andrew Bowie
THE GHETTO Bryan Cheyette
GLACIATION David J. A. Evans
GLOBAL CATASTROPHES Bill McGuire
GLOBAL ECONOMIC HISTORY Robert C. Allen
GLOBAL ISLAM Nile Green
GLOBALIZATION Manfred B. Steger
GOD John Bowker
GOETHE Ritchie Robertson
THE GOTHIC Nick Groom
GOVERNANCE Mark Bevir
GRAVITY Timothy Clifton
THE GREAT DEPRESSION AND THE NEW DEAL Eric Rauchway
HABEAS CORPUS Amanda Tyler
HABERMAS James Gordon Finlayson
THE HABSBURG EMPIRE Martyn Rady
HAPPINESS Daniel M. Haybron
THE HARLEM RENAISSANCE Cheryl A. Wall
THE HEBREW BIBLE AS LITERATURE Tod Linafelt
HEGEL Peter Singer
HEIDEGGER Michael Inwood
THE HELLENISTIC AGE Peter Thonemann
HEREDITY John Waller
HERMENEUTICS Jens Zimmermann
HERODOTUS Jennifer T. Roberts
HIEROGLYPHS Penelope Wilson
HINDUISM Kim Knott
HISTORY John H. Arnold
THE HISTORY OF ASTRONOMY Michael Hoskin
THE HISTORY OF CHEMISTRY William H. Brock
THE HISTORY OF CHILDHOOD James Marten
THE HISTORY OF CINEMA Geoffrey Nowell-Smith
THE HISTORY OF LIFE Michael Benton
THE HISTORY OF MATHEMATICS Jacqueline Stedall
THE HISTORY OF MEDICINE William Bynum
THE HISTORY OF PHYSICS J. L. Heilbron
THE HISTORY OF TIME Leofranc Holford-Strevens
HIV AND AIDS Alan Whiteside
HOBBES Richard Tuck
HOLLYWOOD Peter Decherney
THE HOLY ROMAN EMPIRE Joachim Whaley
HOME Michael Allen Fox
HOMER Barbara Graziosi
HORMONES Martin Luck
HORROR Darryl Jones
HUMAN ANATOMY Leslie Klenerman
HUMAN EVOLUTION Bernard Wood
HUMAN PHYSIOLOGY Jamie A. Davies
HUMAN RIGHTS Andrew Clapham
HUMANISM Stephen Law
HUME James A. Harris
HUMOUR Noël Carroll
THE ICE AGE Jamie Woodward
IDENTITY Florian Coulmas
IDEOLOGY Michael Freeden
THE IMMUNE SYSTEM Paul Klenerman
INDIAN CINEMA Ashish Rajadhyaksha
INDIAN PHILOSOPHY Sue Hamilton
THE INDUSTRIAL REVOLUTION Robert C. Allen
INFECTIOUS DISEASE Marta L. Wayne and Benjamin M. Bolker
INFINITY Ian Stewart
INFORMATION Luciano Floridi
INNOVATION Mark Dodgson and David Gann

INTELLECTUAL PROPERTY
Siva Vaidhyanathan
INTELLIGENCE Ian J. Deary
INTERNATIONAL LAW
Vaughan Lowe
INTERNATIONAL MIGRATION
Khalid Koser
INTERNATIONAL RELATIONS
Christian Reus-Smit
INTERNATIONAL SECURITY
Christopher S. Browning
IRAN Ali M. Ansari
ISLAM Malise Ruthven
ISLAMIC HISTORY Adam Silverstein
ISLAMIC LAW Mashood A. Baderin
ISOTOPES Rob Ellam
ITALIAN LITERATURE
Peter Hainsworth and David Robey
HENRY JAMES Susan L. Mizruchi
JESUS Richard Bauckham
JEWISH HISTORY David N. Myers
JEWISH LITERATURE Ilan Stavans
JOURNALISM Ian Hargreaves
JAMES JOYCE Colin MacCabe
JUDAISM Norman Solomon
JUNG Anthony Stevens
KABBALAH Joseph Dan
KAFKA Ritchie Robertson
KANT Roger Scruton
KEYNES Robert Skidelsky
KIERKEGAARD Patrick Gardiner
KNOWLEDGE Jennifer Nagel
THE KORAN Michael Cook
KOREA Michael J. Seth
LAKES Warwick F. Vincent
LANDSCAPE ARCHITECTURE
Ian H. Thompson
LANDSCAPES AND GEOMORPHOLOGY
Andrew Goudie and Heather Viles
LANGUAGES Stephen R. Anderson
LATE ANTIQUITY Gillian Clark
LAW Raymond Wacks
THE LAWS OF THERMODYNAMICS
Peter Atkins
LEADERSHIP Keith Grint
LEARNING Mark Haselgrove
LEIBNIZ Maria Rosa Antognazza
C. S. LEWIS James Como
LIBERALISM Michael Freeden
LIGHT Ian Walmsley
LINCOLN Allen C. Guelzo
LINGUISTICS Peter Matthews
LITERARY THEORY Jonathan Culler
LOCKE John Dunn
LOGIC Graham Priest
LOVE Ronald de Sousa
MARTIN LUTHER Scott H. Hendrix
MACHIAVELLI Quentin Skinner
MADNESS Andrew Scull
MAGIC Owen Davies
MAGNA CARTA Nicholas Vincent
MAGNETISM Stephen Blundell
MALTHUS Donald Winch
MAMMALS T. S. Kemp
MANAGEMENT John Hendry
NELSON MANDELA Elleke Boehmer
MAO Delia Davin
MARINE BIOLOGY Philip V. Mladenov
MARKETING
Kenneth Le Meunier-FitzHugh
THE MARQUIS DE SADE John Phillips
MARTYRDOM Jolyon Mitchell
MARX Peter Singer
MATERIALS Christopher Hall
MATHEMATICAL FINANCE
Mark H. A. Davis
MATHEMATICS Timothy Gowers
MATTER Geoff Cottrell
THE MAYA Matthew Restall and Amara Solari
THE MEANING OF LIFE
Terry Eagleton
MEASUREMENT David Hand
MEDICAL ETHICS Michael Dunn and Tony Hope
MEDICAL LAW Charles Foster
MEDIEVAL BRITAIN John Gillingham and Ralph A. Griffiths
MEDIEVAL LITERATURE
Elaine Treharne
MEDIEVAL PHILOSOPHY
John Marenbon
MEMORY Jonathan K. Foster
METAPHYSICS Stephen Mumford
METHODISM William J. Abraham
THE MEXICAN REVOLUTION
Alan Knight
MICROBIOLOGY Nicholas P. Money
MICROECONOMICS Avinash Dixit

MICROSCOPY Terence Allen
THE MIDDLE AGES Miri Rubin
MILITARY JUSTICE Eugene R. Fidell
MILITARY STRATEGY
Antulio J. Echevarria II
MINERALS David Vaughan
MIRACLES Yujin Nagasawa
MODERN ARCHITECTURE
Adam Sharr
MODERN ART David Cottington
MODERN BRAZIL Anthony W. Pereira
MODERN CHINA Rana Mitter
MODERN DRAMA
Kirsten E. Shepherd-Barr
MODERN FRANCE
Vanessa R. Schwartz
MODERN INDIA Craig Jeffrey
MODERN IRELAND Senia Pašeta
MODERN ITALY Anna Cento Bull
MODERN JAPAN Christopher
Goto-Jones
MODERN LATIN AMERICAN
LITERATURE
Roberto González Echevarría
MODERN WAR Richard English
MODERNISM Christopher Butler
MOLECULAR BIOLOGY Aysha Divan
and Janice A. Royds
MOLECULES Philip Ball
MONASTICISM Stephen J. Davis
THE MONGOLS Morris Rossabi
MONTAIGNE William M. Hamlin
MOONS David A. Rothery
MORMONISM Richard Lyman Bushman
MOUNTAINS Martin F. Price
MUHAMMAD Jonathan A. C. Brown
MULTICULTURALISM Ali Rattansi
MULTILINGUALISM John C. Maher
MUSIC Nicholas Cook
MYTH Robert A. Segal
NAPOLEON David Bell
THE NAPOLEONIC WARS
Mike Rapport
NATIONALISM Steven Grosby
NATIVE AMERICAN LITERATURE
Sean Teuton
NAVIGATION Jim Bennett
NAZI GERMANY Jane Caplan
NEOLIBERALISM Manfred B. Steger
and Ravi K. Roy
NETWORKS Guido Caldarelli and
Michele Catanzaro
THE NEW TESTAMENT
Luke Timothy Johnson
THE NEW TESTAMENT AS
LITERATURE Kyle Keefer
NEWTON Robert Iliffe
NIELS BOHR J. L. Heilbron
NIETZSCHE Michael Tanner
NINETEENTH-CENTURY BRITAIN
Christopher Harvie and
H. C. G. Matthew
THE NORMAN CONQUEST
George Garnett
NORTH AMERICAN INDIANS
Theda Perdue and Michael D. Green
NORTHERN IRELAND
Marc Mulholland
NOTHING Frank Close
NUCLEAR PHYSICS Frank Close
NUCLEAR POWER Maxwell Irvine
NUCLEAR WEAPONS
Joseph M. Siracusa
NUMBER THEORY Robin Wilson
NUMBERS Peter M. Higgins
NUTRITION David A. Bender
OBJECTIVITY Stephen Gaukroger
OCEANS Dorrik Stow
THE OLD TESTAMENT
Michael D. Coogan
THE ORCHESTRA D. Kern Holoman
ORGANIC CHEMISTRY
Graham Patrick
ORGANIZATIONS Mary Jo Hatch
ORGANIZED CRIME
Georgios A. Antonopoulos and
Georgios Papanicolaou
ORTHODOX CHRISTIANITY
A. Edward Siecienski
OVID Llewelyn Morgan
PAGANISM Owen Davies
THE PALESTINIAN-ISRAELI
CONFLICT Martin Bunton
PANDEMICS Christian W. McMillen
PARTICLE PHYSICS Frank Close
PAUL E. P. Sanders
PEACE Oliver P. Richmond
PENTECOSTALISM William K. Kay
PERCEPTION Brian Rogers
THE PERIODIC TABLE Eric R. Scerri

PHILOSOPHICAL METHOD Timothy Williamson
PHILOSOPHY Edward Craig
PHILOSOPHY IN THE ISLAMIC WORLD Peter Adamson
PHILOSOPHY OF BIOLOGY Samir Okasha
PHILOSOPHY OF LAW Raymond Wacks
PHILOSOPHY OF PHYSICS David Wallace
PHILOSOPHY OF SCIENCE Samir Okasha
PHILOSOPHY OF RELIGION Tim Bayne
PHOTOGRAPHY Steve Edwards
PHYSICAL CHEMISTRY Peter Atkins
PHYSICS Sidney Perkowitz
PILGRIMAGE Ian Reader
PLAGUE Paul Slack
PLANETS David A. Rothery
PLANTS Timothy Walker
PLATE TECTONICS Peter Molnar
PLATO Julia Annas
POETRY Bernard O'Donoghue
POLITICAL PHILOSOPHY David Miller
POLITICS Kenneth Minogue
POPULISM Cas Mudde and Cristóbal Rovira Kaltwasser
POSTCOLONIALISM Robert Young
POSTMODERNISM Christopher Butler
POSTSTRUCTURALISM Catherine Belsey
POVERTY Philip N. Jefferson
PREHISTORY Chris Gosden
PRESOCRATIC PHILOSOPHY Catherine Osborne
PRIVACY Raymond Wacks
PROBABILITY John Haigh
PROGRESSIVISM Walter Nugent
PROHIBITION W. J. Rorabaugh
PROJECTS Andrew Davies
PROTESTANTISM Mark A. Noll
PSYCHIATRY Tom Burns
PSYCHOANALYSIS Daniel Pick
PSYCHOLOGY Gillian Butler and Freda McManus
PSYCHOLOGY OF MUSIC Elizabeth Hellmuth Margulis
PSYCHOPATHY Essi Viding
PSYCHOTHERAPY Tom Burns and Eva Burns-Lundgren
PUBLIC ADMINISTRATION Stella Z. Theodoulou and Ravi K. Roy
PUBLIC HEALTH Virginia Berridge
PURITANISM Francis J. Bremer
THE QUAKERS Pink Dandelion
QUANTUM THEORY John Polkinghorne
RACISM Ali Rattansi
RADIOACTIVITY Claudio Tuniz
RASTAFARI Ennis B. Edmonds
READING Belinda Jack
THE REAGAN REVOLUTION Gil Troy
REALITY Jan Westerhoff
RECONSTRUCTION Allen C. Guelzo
THE REFORMATION Peter Marshall
REFUGEES Gil Loescher
RELATIVITY Russell Stannard
RELIGION Thomas A. Tweed
RELIGION IN AMERICA Timothy Beal
THE RENAISSANCE Jerry Brotton
RENAISSANCE ART Geraldine A. Johnson
RENEWABLE ENERGY Nick Jelley
REPTILES T.S. Kemp
REVOLUTIONS Jack A. Goldstone
RHETORIC Richard Toye
RISK Baruch Fischhoff and John Kadvany
RITUAL Barry Stephenson
RIVERS Nick Middleton
ROBOTICS Alan Winfield
ROCKS Jan Zalasiewicz
ROMAN BRITAIN Peter Salway
THE ROMAN EMPIRE Christopher Kelly
THE ROMAN REPUBLIC David M. Gwynn
ROMANTICISM Michael Ferber
ROUSSEAU Robert Wokler
RUSSELL A. C. Grayling
THE RUSSIAN ECONOMY Richard Connolly
RUSSIAN HISTORY Geoffrey Hosking
RUSSIAN LITERATURE Catriona Kelly
THE RUSSIAN REVOLUTION S. A. Smith
SAINTS Simon Yarrow
SAMURAI Michael Wert
SAVANNAS Peter A. Furley

SCEPTICISM Duncan Pritchard
SCHIZOPHRENIA Chris Frith and Eve Johnstone
SCHOPENHAUER Christopher Janaway
SCIENCE AND RELIGION Thomas Dixon
SCIENCE FICTION David Seed
THE SCIENTIFIC REVOLUTION Lawrence M. Principe
SCOTLAND Rab Houston
SECULARISM Andrew Copson
SEXUAL SELECTION Marlene Zuk and Leigh W. Simmons
SEXUALITY Véronique Mottier
WILLIAM SHAKESPEARE Stanley Wells
SHAKESPEARE'S COMEDIES Bart van Es
SHAKESPEARE'S SONNETS AND POEMS Jonathan F. S. Post
SHAKESPEARE'S TRAGEDIES Stanley Wells
GEORGE BERNARD SHAW Christopher Wixson
THE SHORT STORY Andrew Kahn
SIKHISM Eleanor Nesbitt
SILENT FILM Donna Kornhaber
THE SILK ROAD James A. Millward
SLANG Jonathon Green
SLEEP Steven W. Lockley and Russell G. Foster
SMELL Matthew Cobb
ADAM SMITH Christopher J. Berry
SOCIAL AND CULTURAL ANTHROPOLOGY John Monaghan and Peter Just
SOCIAL PSYCHOLOGY Richard J. Crisp
SOCIAL WORK Sally Holland and Jonathan Scourfield
SOCIALISM Michael Newman
SOCIOLINGUISTICS John Edwards
SOCIOLOGY Steve Bruce
SOCRATES C. C. W. Taylor
SOFT MATTER Tom McLeish
SOUND Mike Goldsmith
SOUTHEAST ASIA James R. Rush
THE SOVIET UNION Stephen Lovell
THE SPANISH CIVIL WAR Helen Graham
SPANISH LITERATURE Jo Labanyi
SPINOZA Roger Scruton
SPIRITUALITY Philip Sheldrake
SPORT Mike Cronin
STARS Andrew King
STATISTICS David J. Hand
STEM CELLS Jonathan Slack
STOICISM Brad Inwood
STRUCTURAL ENGINEERING David Blockley
STUART BRITAIN John Morrill
THE SUN Philip Judge
SUPERCONDUCTIVITY Stephen Blundell
SUPERSTITION Stuart Vyse
SYMMETRY Ian Stewart
SYNAESTHESIA Julia Simner
SYNTHETIC BIOLOGY Jamie A. Davies
SYSTEMS BIOLOGY Eberhard O. Voit
TAXATION Stephen Smith
TEETH Peter S. Ungar
TELESCOPES Geoff Cottrell
TERRORISM Charles Townshend
THEATRE Marvin Carlson
THEOLOGY David F. Ford
THINKING AND REASONING Jonathan St B. T. Evans
THOUGHT Tim Bayne
TIBETAN BUDDHISM Matthew T. Kapstein
TIDES David George Bowers and Emyr Martyn Roberts
TIME Jenann Ismael
TOCQUEVILLE Harvey C. Mansfield
LEO TOLSTOY Liza Knapp
TOPOLOGY Richard Earl
TRAGEDY Adrian Poole
TRANSLATION Matthew Reynolds
THE TREATY OF VERSAILLES Michael S. Neiberg
TRIGONOMETRY Glen Van Brummelen
THE TROJAN WAR Eric H. Cline
TRUST Katherine Hawley
THE TUDORS John Guy
TWENTIETH-CENTURY BRITAIN Kenneth O. Morgan
TYPOGRAPHY Paul Luna
THE UNITED NATIONS Jussi M. Hanhimäki

UNIVERSITIES AND COLLEGES David Palfreyman and Paul Temple
THE U.S. CIVIL WAR Louis P. Masur
THE U.S. CONGRESS Donald A. Ritchie
THE U.S. CONSTITUTION David J. Bodenhamer
THE U.S. SUPREME COURT Linda Greenhouse
UTILITARIANISM Katarzyna de Lazari-Radek and Peter Singer
UTOPIANISM Lyman Tower Sargent
VETERINARY SCIENCE James Yeates
THE VIKINGS Julian D. Richards
THE VIRGIN MARY Mary Joan Winn Leith
THE VIRTUES Craig A. Boyd and Kevin Timpe
VIRUSES Dorothy H. Crawford
VOLCANOES Michael J. Branney and Jan Zalasiewicz
VOLTAIRE Nicholas Cronk
WAR AND RELIGION Jolyon Mitchell and Joshua Rey
WAR AND TECHNOLOGY Alex Roland
WATER John Finney
WAVES Mike Goldsmith
WEATHER Storm Dunlop
THE WELFARE STATE David Garland
WITCHCRAFT Malcolm Gaskill
WITTGENSTEIN A. C. Grayling
WORK Stephen Fineman
WORLD MUSIC Philip Bohlman
THE WORLD TRADE ORGANIZATION Amrita Narlikar
WORLD WAR II Gerhard L. Weinberg
WRITING AND SCRIPT Andrew Robinson
ZIONISM Michael Stanislawski
ÉMILE ZOLA Brian Nelson

Available soon:

PHILOSOPHY OF MIND Barbara Gail Montero
JANE AUSTEN Tom Keymer
PAKISTAN Pippa Virdee
PLANETARY SYSTEMS Raymond T. Pierrehumbert
THE HISTORY OF POLITICAL THOUGHT Richard Whatmore

Andrew Kahn

THE SHORT STORY

A Very Short Introduction

Great Clarendon Street, Oxford, OX2 6DP,
United Kingdom

Oxford University Press is a department of the University of Oxford. It furthers the University's objective of excellence in research, scholarship, and education by publishing worldwide. Oxford is a registered trade mark of Oxford University Press in the UK and in certain other countries

First edition published in 2021

Impression: 1

Published in the United States of America by Oxford University Press
198 Madison Avenue, New York, NY 10016, United States of America

British Library Cataloguing in Publication Data
Data available

Library of Congress Control Number: 2021940310

ISBN 978-0-19-875463-3

Printed in Great Britain by
Ashford Colour Press Ltd, Gosport, Hampshire

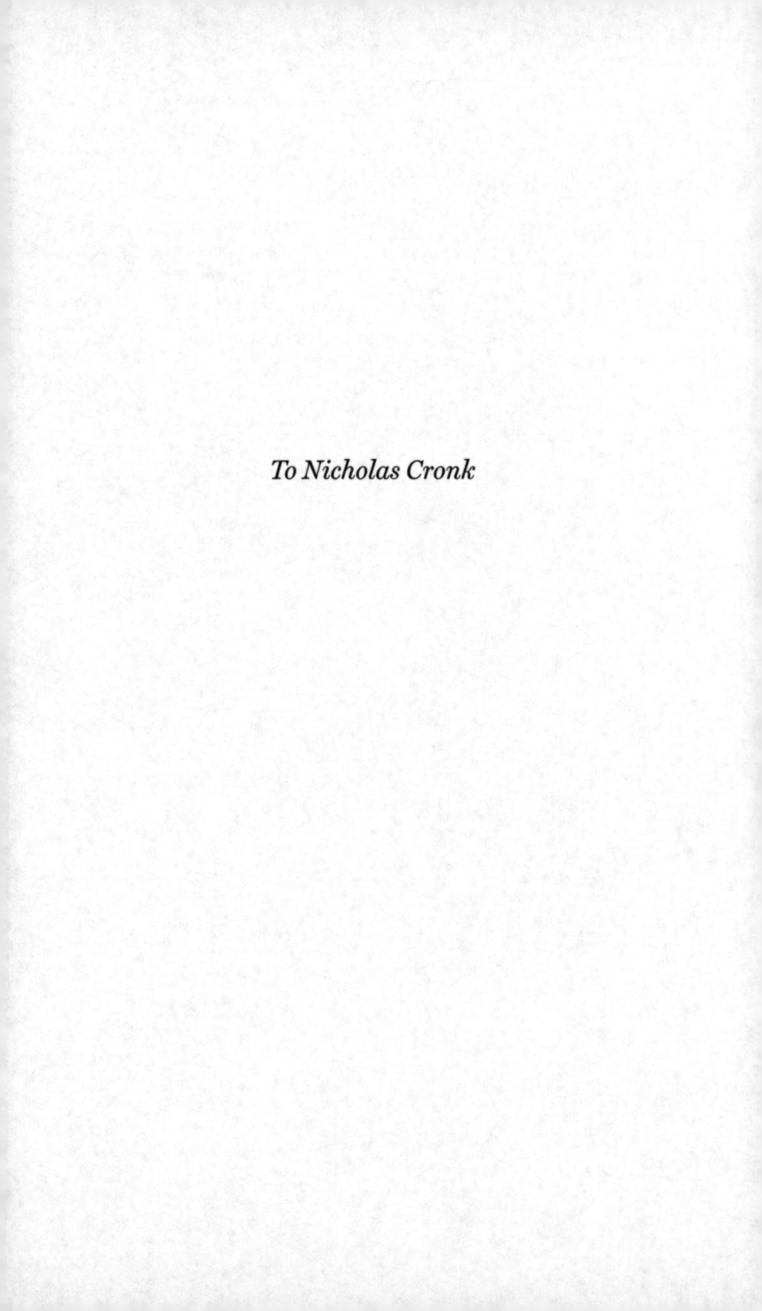

To Nicholas Cronk

Contents

Preface xix

Acknowledgements xxvii

List of illustrations xxix

1 The rise of the short story 1

2 Openings 16

3 Voices 30

4 Place 48

5 The plot thickens...and thins 64

6 Ironies and reversals 81

7 Chekhov's heirs 94

8 Endings 107

References 119

Further reading 129

Index 137

Preface

When the Canadian author Alice Munro won the Nobel Prize for Literature in 2013, the first to be awarded to a writer exclusively of short stories, she commented, 'I would really hope this would make people see the short story as an important art, not just something you played around with until you got a novel.' If the genre looks like a poor (albeit loved) literary relation to the novel that may reflect a widespread belief that anyone can tell stories because as a species we are hard-wired to invent or tell them. When asked what it took to make plot, characterization, description and prose come together satisfactorily, Munro answered, 'hard work', and spoke of a more difficult 'job than she expected', a comment that drily balances out both the expectation that telling stories should come naturally and that telling stories is a highly skilled craft (Figure 1).

The job of defining theoretically and practically what the short story is has become harder because the genre has been raising its game for well over a century and also gone global. For much of the 20th century, there was a commonplace view that the lives of their people inclined certain national literary traditions—above all, the Irish, Americans, and Russians—to excel in the form. Bibliographies from the 1930s to the 1980s are rife with titles promoting the story as a proxy for national history. Frank O'Connor's *The Lonely Voice* (1962), a seminal work of criticism by

Can You Write SHORT STORIES?

Short story writing is the ideal hobby. Learn the essential technique by post—the Regent way. In a fascinating course you are shown how to get plots, how to construct, and how and where to sell MSS.

Post this advertisement to The Regent Institute (Dept. LJ/19A), Palace Gate, London, W.8, for a free prospectus, "How to Succeed as a Writer." There is no obligation. **Send for this interesting booklet NOW.**

NAME..

ADDRESS...

....

1. William Lawton in *The Dial* (1897): 'Every sort of originality, especially in the short story, is eagerly caught at. The market seems enormous, production is entirely too much encouraged.'

a great practitioner of the short story, was also emphatic about the connection between the genre and Irishness. His argument was largely class-based, holding that peoples who had suffered social exclusion, whether through poverty or colonization, provided a pool of marginal characters (or in Russian 'the little people') best suited to short narratives. 'A national art form,' says Richard Ford, 'the blessed Irish genre', says Joyce Carol Oates, although Anne Enright, an anthologist as well as short story writer, clearly sees the notion that there is an Irishness to stories written in Ireland as bluff. Once nourished by rural themes, even the Irish story has grown to encompass city-dwellers (as can be seen in Chapter 5's discussion of a story by John McGahern) and much more diverse populations as well as the Irish diaspora. There has been a related perception that despite its great tradition of the novel, English writers have been less successful as story writers. That view has been tackled head on by A. S. Byatt in the Introduction to her *Oxford Book of English Stories*, and readers can turn to collections by Julian Barnes (*Pulse*, 2011), Claire-Louise Bennett (*Pond*, 2015), and Frances Leviston's acclaimed *The Voice in my Ear* (2020) or any of the three volumes edited by Philip Hensher to see the myth of English uninterest vigorously belied by a cross-generational spirit of innovation gripping the form across centuries in the 1900s and the 2000s.

But more generally, globalization and translation have opened up and stimulated other traditions. It may be the compact scale of the form, necessarily shorter than the novel, that gives the genre its cosmopolitan passport. The short story has come to be seen as a universal type of fiction well suited to an age of 'world literature' and notably engaged with social reality, including gender and ethnic issues, themes of substance that survive linguistic and cultural translation especially well in a globalized world (Figure 2). The definition of short story writing in national or geographic terms (e.g. as American, Russian, English, Irish, South American) has in recent decades yielded to an internationalized market. One indicator of change can be found in the work published in

The New Yorker magazine. Unrivalled in the longevity and distinction of its commitment to the form, a cradle of the great mid-century British and American tradition and home to fabled names such as Capote, Welty, Spark, Cheever, Trevor, and many others, the magazine remains an active incubator for the best of short story writing. From at least the 2000s the magazine has broken out of what had perhaps fossilized into a special type of 'New Yorker' story, sometimes lampooned as plotless albeit superbly written, into a space that is culturally more diverse and mainstream. International anthologies are just as prominent as national ones, and when a national anthology appears it can be far from parochial: for example, the *Penguin Book of Italian Short Stories* (2019) is edited by Jhumpa Lahiri, an American author born in London of Bengali parentage, now living in Rome.

For authors and readers alike, plot was once the be-all and end-all. In the age of the magazine (treated in Chapter 1) stories were generally written to formula to please with a neat twist, leading to criticisms that plot had achieved a mechanical regularity. In the 19th and early 20th centuries, newspaper layout determined the word count of a story. As tales found outlets in quality reviews, anthologies, and eventually single-author collections, they became stories, generally longer and more crafted without nevertheless becoming wannabe novels. The shape of the story has been continually reworked to explore inner and outer realities through linkages of psychology and motivation, situation and history, character and destiny. Serious writers of literary short stories, like practitioners of serious novels, are able to create the illusion that their characters are independent agents free to make their choices outside the plot-driven choices of the author. Their stories express the complex relation of human identity and individual situation to the world, subjected to the norms of the art.

It seems usual to define the short story by comparison with the novel and, above all, to give priority to length as the thing that distinguishes the two. A short story is not a short novel, nor is it

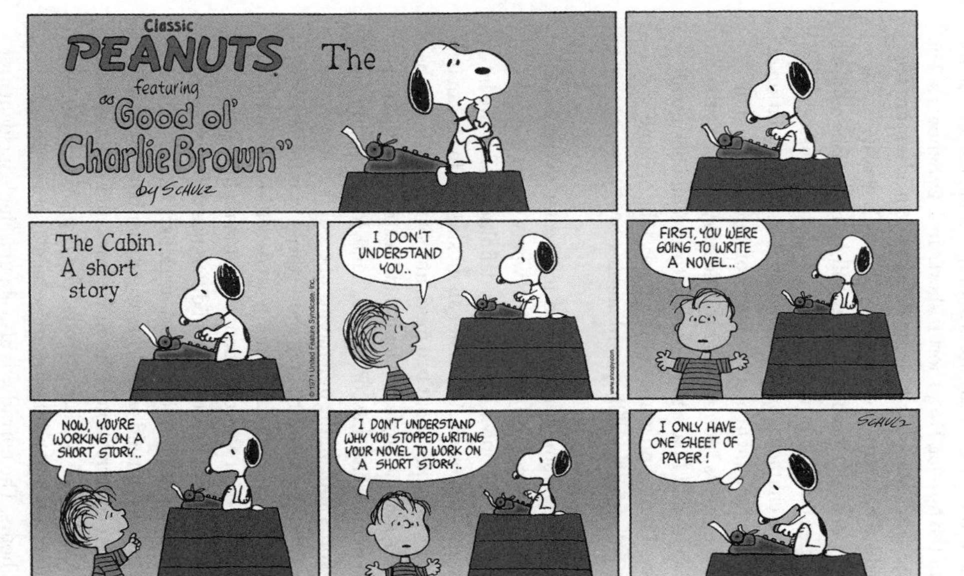

2. V. S. Pritchett on Katherine Mansfield, 'One spoke of the "art of the short story" as one might speak of the "art" of the sonnet or madrigal; for the short story had ceased to be an anecdote or novel in brief.'

merely a joke. Attempts have regularly been made to draw distinctions between the sketch, anecdote, and novella, and there have been further strenuous efforts to differentiate the long short story from the novella. How short is short? In J. D. Salinger's 'The Laughing Man', a story partly about being told an adventure tale, the embedded narrative is described as having 'a classic dimension' because it 'tended to sprawl all over the place, and yet it remained essentially portable'. In Helen Garner's 'Postcards from Surfers' a character makes the point about the relaxation of the classical containment and symmetry of plot construction when she comments, 'Sometimes my little story overflows the available space and I have to run over onto a second postcard. This means I must find a smaller, secondary tale, or some disconnected remark, to fill up card number two.'

The length of short stories mentioned and treated in this book extends, at the shorter end, from about twenty words to about 8,000, probably the upper limit on any definition before we hit the short novel or novella. The point about size and focus can be illustrated by thinking about two much anthologized American stories, each about a single incident, that illustrate expectations about size defined either as, on the one hand, length or number of pages or words and, on the other, unity of event that moves the boundary from short toward long short story. Dorothy Parker's 'Here We Are' captures a pair of newly-weds setting off on their honeymoon by train. Nervous about their first night together, they discover, as they chat, more points of difference than agreement, and then draw back from their smart-aleck barbs into civility. The story leaves much unsaid as the characters spar out of sexual tension. Their conversation is the entire story, and about as long as a single section of William Styron's 'The Long March' (1952), an account of a brutal military exercise held over a period of thirty-six hours. The narrative is also about a single incident, but Styron uses its scale to build portraits of his two main characters, locked in enmity and seen through the eyes of a more neutral narrator.

The restriction of the short story to single incidents, whether banal or moments of poetic intensity, is the traditional strength of unity of action that Edgar Allan Poe, a pioneer in the genre, identified as essential to its practice. Unity more than scale is a defining criterion. Elizabeth Bowen, the much-admired Anglo-Irish author of nearly a dozen separate collections, maintained that 'stories, unlike novels, are a matter of vision rather than feeling', by which she meant that the vision is complete in itself. This has something in common with the appreciation of one critic for how Edith Wharton in her stories 'removed the veils that are spread over most lives and by wont and custom conceal the inner workings from the eyes of all but a few; it is the privilege of the artist to penetrate their enveloping folds and scan the bare souls within'. There was no subject beyond Italo Calvino's playful imagination and gift for formal invention whether in the novel or in the twelve short stories on sci-fi themes he published in 1969 as *Cosmicomics*. When writing about his experience of the Second World War as an adolescent, Italo Calvino created a trilogy of realist stories (*Into the War*, 1954) over a unitary form. The transition from adolescence to youth 'might have been a theme for a novel', but the linked stories, all featuring the same protagonist, permitted a gradualism to the self-portrait, each story 'modulated according to its own state of mind and its own rhythm'.

There are states of being and mind, such as rapture, loneliness, and grief, where the short story, like the poem, is proportionally suited to emotional intensity. Another example of a book serving as an umbrella for separate but linked accounts is Yuko Tsushima's *Territory of Light*, a touching feminist Japanese narrative, influenced by Tennessee Williams's work, of a single mother and daughter first published as separate chapters and then as the novel. All these examples give proof of Helen Simpson's claim that the 'short story form is particularly good for uncomfortable or edgy subjects'. And, incidentally, they indirectly expose O'Connor's argument about the class of short story protagonists as more valid observation than iron-rule since none of the protagonists in the works just mentioned qualifies as down and out.

Stories can also achieve larger vistas as parts of a cycle or thematically linked book. In the six books of stories written about the Soviet labour camps, the Russian master Varlaam Shalamov, whose influences include Chekhov, Maupassant, and Proust, brought together dozens of stories, the shortest being a prose poem of a single page, the longest rarely exceeding fifteen pages, all set in the bleakest of worlds; and while few characters survive across the entire *Kolyma Tales*, the stories share recurring themes such as the meaning of work, the feeling of hunger and cold, treachery, and hope, and are on such a scale that individual convicts stand for types and types gain individuality. Part and whole can therefore stand separately and cumulatively—or sequentially, as in the case of John Updike's eighteen *Maple Stories*, which capture marriage, American style, starting in the 1970s, by telling the histories of a single couple, Richard and Joan Maple, over twenty years, or the seven stories about the struggles of black women that Gloria Naylor united as *The Women of Brewster Place* (1982), arguably more cycle than novel.

The present book is not a potted history of the genre, nor is it a book strictly speaking about rules or an endorsement of a total theory of the short story. Through some survey and mainly close reading of stories that have a representative quality, it explores how a set of forms, structures, and themes common to the genre across national boundaries combine and recombine to give the genre a protean life. It aims, furthermore, to suggest how, within such a brief compass, the short story can achieve big things like imitating reality, bringing characters to life, intimating universal concerns, elaborating and revising social and gender stereotypes, offering comic relief, and delivering an emotional experience.

Acknowledgements

Writing a short book on a short literary form with a vast and rich history has been a challenge and delight, and I am grateful to Andrea Keegan and Luciana O'Flaherty for taking the project forward in the VSI series and to OUP editorial and production for all manner of help. Friends and colleagues will be relieved now that I can desist from asking, 'Who is your favourite short story writer?' or the like. For advice on content and comments on drafts I am grateful to Daniel Altshuler, Tom Ball, Nicholas Cronk, Bethan Davies (of the Rothermere Institute, University of Oxford), Adam Frank, Allan Hepburn, Michael Jonik, Judith Luna, Lulu Miller, Robin Miller, Gretty Mirdal, Jacqueline Norton, Marguerite Pigeon, Gillian Pink, Oliver Ready, and Seth Whidden.

List of illustrations

1 William Lawton in *The Dial* (1897): 'Every sort of originality, especially in the short story, is eagerly caught at. The market seems enormous, production is entirely too much encouraged.' **xx**

'Can You Write Short Stories?' *The Listener*, vol. 49, no. 1252, 26 Feb. 1953, p. 368 courtesy of *The Listener* 1953.

2 V. S. Pritchett on Katherine Mansfield, 'One spoke of the "art of the short story" as one might speak of the "art" of the sonnet or madrigal; for the short story had ceased to be an anecdote or novel in brief.' **xxiii**

PEANUTS ©1971 Peanuts Worldwide LLC. Dist. By ANDREWS MCMEEL SYNDICATION. Reprinted with permission. All rights reserved.

3 'The symptoms of the journalized short story are easily distinguished . . . An overplus of "body" is probably a symptom.' Letter from a reader to *The Dial*, 1929. **6**

Retro Ad Archives / Alamy Stock Photo.

4 Edwin Muir in *The Listener*, 'There are signs that the story is becoming more popular again.' **14**

'Make your Pen Pay for your Holiday!' *The Listener*, vol. 43, no. 1107, 13 Apr. 1950, p. 672 courtesy of *The Listener* 1950.

List of Illustrations

Chapter 1
The rise of the short story

The rise of the short story from the Industrial Age occurred largely in the context of British and American print culture. That development traces a long arc from the establishment of the genre as a staple of 19th-century newspapers and magazines to its autonomy as a mode of literature held to be on par with the novel. In the 19th century, globally from Australia to Russia, the short story catered to the taste of growing readerships for entertainment, and its brevity and easy supply appealed to editors. Readers and publishers alike were avid for lively incident that could be compressed into the short space of one or more columns on a page. The account in this chapter, moving from the 19th-century magazine origins of the short story to its debated status in the literary field, reminds us of its popular origins, its style and low prestige dictated by the literary marketplace before a new appreciation of the form's intrinsic possibilities eventually attracted artistic ambition and earned it critical value.

'Read all about it!': newspaper stories

Massive growth in readerships for newspapers and magazines owing to the availability of cheap paper and advances in printing was a global phenomenon in the 19th century. While the period also saw the increasing professionalization of authorship, storytelling was a popular phenomenon. For much of the 19th century, readers could find short fictions as well as 'true-life' tales first on the pages of newspapers and later in magazines that increasingly carved out a niche for fiction. The word 'story' often signified any narrative, real or invented, in the American, British, and French periodical press. What mattered most in placing a story in print was its shape (beginning, middle, end) and believable and familiar content ('recital of matters of fact', 'use of materials already employed', as the *Bath Chronicle* put it).

Readers liked the boundary between fiction and non-fiction to be porous, narrative to be carried by the voice of the storyteller, and interest sustained by topicality. Tales recounted from experience were the stock-in-trade of magazines and newspapers, including eyewitness accounts of exotic travels or brave exploits. Whether the incident reported was experienced directly by the author or overheard, the reader had to believe in its occurrence. As early as the 1820s, the English author Elizabeth Inchbald (1753–1821), already admired for her novels, saw her collections of tales praised in *The Literary Examiner* 'for a singularly direct power of narrative, which carries forwards the incidents' and her 'compactness of conception in character and plot'. 'Hot off the presses' applies nearly as much to tales of the everyday as it did to actual news stories. 'At 8 a.m. it lay on Giuseppi's news-stand, still damp from the presses' is how the ever popular O. Henry began his classic 'A Newspaper Story'. *The American Ladies' Magazine*, which boasted of its original tales, was typical in printing stories like 'The Mechanic's Wife' (1842) about a transaction between a shopkeeper and a housewife getting by on credit. Content crossed borders of different kinds. Over two issues in November 1869, the *Saturday Evening Post* printed 'The Disappearance of John Ackland', a shocker by Robert Bulwer-Lytton that had originally appeared in Charles Dickens's magazine *All The Year Round* (Sept.–Oct. 1869). On its republication it carried in bold type the tag: 'A TRUE STORY.'

The pool of authors was swollen by amateurs, presumably lured by the attraction of being in print, since publishers kept fees low. Edgar Allan Poe earned a modest four or five dollars per page; eventually, as advertising enhanced their revenue, magazines would pay authors more. Re-publication was one way to respond to the need for content. Many newspapers in Britain and the United States even expanded their offering of fiction by providing periodic round-ups of short stories published elsewhere. *The Caledonian Mercury* of January 1840, for example, surveyed recent short story publications not only from competitors but from anthologies such as *Bentley's Miscellany*, singling out Poe's 'The Murders in the Rue Morgue' (1841) because it 'completely floored our gravity'. Republication was a regular occurrence in American magazines until 1845, when copyright laws offered domestic (but not international) authors protection. A world away in thinly populated Australia, readers depended on foreign imports for novels. Yet newspapers did commission stories from Australian authors, both short and mostly longer, and well over 7,000 short fictions have been identified in the country's 19th-century newspapers. These stories reflected Australian life, including sometimes positive portrayals of Aboriginals in defiance of colonial stereotypes.

Entertainment was an important factor. No one doubted that life was stranger than fiction, and readers were hooked on reading all about it. Lurid stories stylized as Gothic tales regularly featured. In local newspapers these could be sightings of ghosts by residents; in more established organs of the press such as the *Derby Mercury*, accounts were more impersonally dressed up as literature. *Stories of a Bride* (under the by-line 'By the Author of "A Mummy"') offered the reader a total experience of 'horror struck expressions', 'gloom', 'apprehensions', all felt by the heroine Adelaide, who in the tale's final line is 'saved' by a bandit. Effect matters more than veracity, provenance, or unity of construction, as the opening paragraph states:

> It is not of much importance what vehicle is used to introduce a series of tales. We therefore hasten, without examining the one which gave the present work its title, to give an interesting scene from one of the 'Stories of a Bride,' called the 'Treasure Seeker'. The heroine, after journeying through a forest in order to approach the prison of her husband, is at length dismayed by the scenes in which she finds herself, and sinks in despair.

In a similar vein, a notice in *The Examiner* in 1827 observed a fashion for a 'certain romantic class of fiction', often expressed in national tales (under discussion were the Irish 'Tales of the O'Hara Family'). These featured action scenes and displays of honour. The *Saturday Evening Post*, originally founded in 1821 and by 1909 America's premier weekly, reproduced a series of accolades from other newspapers about its 'thrilling stories for the family circle'. *Ruddiman Tales and Sketches*, an anthology excerpted in the press, was so bold as to claim that, when well told, books of short stories had many advantages over novels owing to a 'greater variety of subjects, compressed within narrower limits'. A zeal to publish inspired travel, crime, and adventure stories, their fictionality uncertain. Captain Marryat's tales, like Gulliver's, are treated as 'true after the fashion of Homer', according to *The Examiner* (1849): 'It is supposed, or it is a fact, that certain travellers [an English merchant, a botanist, a Spanish poet, a French surgeon, et al.] formed a little institute of their own and meeting periodically at each other's rooms, amused themselves with the production of monthly stories.'

In 1841, a correspondent to the *Saturday Evening Post* opined that owing to the genre's brevity 'the best writers generally will not write short stories... They consider it a waste of time.' Nathaniel Hawthorne notoriously lamented that the 'public taste is presently occupied with trash'. By that time the genre had begun to outgrow the modest number of columns newspapers could allocate, and stories began to follow principles relating to their own artistic composition, less dependent on either oral storytelling or journalistic reporting. The increase in the number of American periodicals that began before the Civil War meant that they reached diverse readerships: from farmers to professionals. Post-bellum growth was far more rapid, thanks to increasing literacy and mechanization of the printing press. Thousands of new periodicals tapped into a large audience of women and children. Sales figures appear to confirm the general thinking that female readerships had a greater appetite for fiction. For example, the *Lady's Home Journal*, founded in 1883, would reach a circulation of about two million by 1912. From the late 19th century until the mid-20th century the short story increasingly became a staple of magazines that diverged according to quality and readership either into elite publications (called 'slicker magazines' or 'slicks' because of their glossy paper) and pulp magazines designed to provide cheap thrills. The rivalry between the two trends would itself become a source of comment as the short story as both a money-spinner and an artistic form gained credibility with editors and authors.

The short story in pulp magazines

In the USA, pulp magazines flourished from the 1920s to 1940s, only to be mostly finished off by a paper and staple shortage during the Second World War, conditions that favoured the survival of more expensive literary magazines. The originator of the pulp magazine was Frank Munsey, who set up as a publisher in New York in the 1880s and made his millions by the 1900s publishing mass fiction in *Munsey*'s and *Argosy's*. His winning formula that 'The story is more important than the paper it is printed on' worked thanks to a supply of cheap wood-pulp paper and a new high-speed printing process. He aimed to beat the weekly newspapers that had treated popular literature as fringe. The polar opposite of quality magazines ('slicks' like *Harper's* and *Scribners*, which were highbrow and more expensive), the pulp magazines (like their earlier British equivalents, the Penny dreadfuls) catered to a mass readership avid for the thrills of action plots full of intrigue, highly sexed men and women, and sometimes violence, available and even affordable during the Depression at a rock-bottom price between five cents and a quarter.

This was the period when the private eye, born in the 1920s, grew into the fictional heroes of Prohibition, hardnosed loners only just on the right side of the law who populated the stories of *Thrilling Detective*, *Ten Detective Aces*, and *Popular Detective* (Figure 3). For ten cents *Dime Detective* provided twelve action-jammed stories.

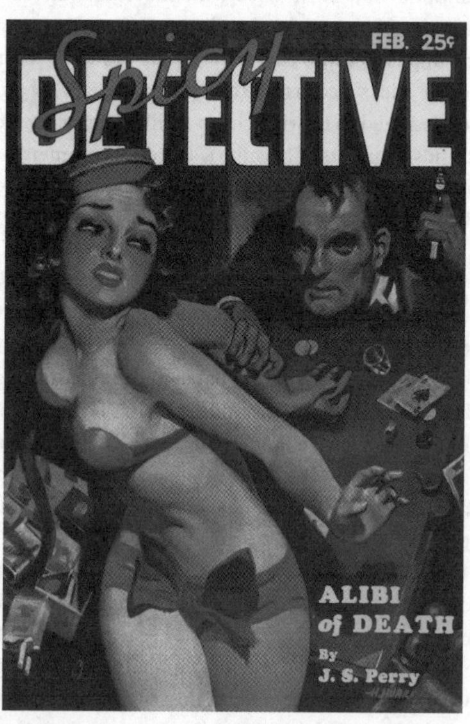

3. 'The symptoms of the journalized short story are easily distinguished . . . An overplus of "body" is probably a symptom.' Letter from a reader to *The Dial*, 1929.

No thrills were better than cheap thrills, and no genre more adaptable than the short story to a variety of plot stratagems. Each weekly normally contained 128 pages and about 120,000 words, with vivid and shocking artwork inside and on the cover. They encompassed a variety of styles or sub-genres of sleuth fictions, detective stories (including confessions), thrillers, adventure (such as westerns), sci-fi, and horror in which nothing could be too breathless (as in the melodramas of *Dime Detective* in the 1930s) or too frivolous (as in the twice monthly *Saucy Stories*) or too lurid (as in works featured in *Spicy Mystery Stories* like Robert Bellem's 'Death's Nocturne' or Arthur Wallace's 'Dungeons for the Blind') or too fantastic (as in the zombies, vampires, and voodoo to be found in *Tales of Magic and Mystery*) or too hard-boiled (the speciality of the cynical sleuths featured in *The Black Mask* whose readership apparently included President Woodrow Wilson).

As in 19th-century newspapers, the pulps also ran 'true stories' and *Detective Tales* had true-life features like the column 'The Crime Clinic'. Munsey's publications included some of the most successful titles such as *Adventure*, *Amazing Stories*, *Black Mask*, *Famous Fantastic Mysteries*, *Ghost Stories*, *Marvel Science Stories*, *Oriental Stories*, *Spicy Mystery Stories*, *Terror Tales*, and *Weird Tales*, and they spawned many competitors, most notably the Clayton Magazines (publishers, among many other crime pulps, of *Clues: A Magazine of Detective Stories*). Many stories were stand-alone, but the magazines also retained their clientele by running serials that reliably delivered to a specific fan-base. *Detective Story Magazine*, which preferred the amateur gumshoe to the hard-boiled sleuth, ran for thirty years as one of the most successful magazines in American history and featured a 'veritable roll-call of crime fiction'. The *Argosy All-Story Weekly* in the 1920s was a pulp magazine that targeted children before finding a more lucrative readership in the 1940s with men's adventure pulp tales and true crime (Susan Glaspell, a popular short story writer, and the true crime pioneer Erle Stanley Gardner both contributed). The *Nick Carter Magazine* in the 1930s set a boyish detective hero of the 1910s well on his way to becoming the secret agent of the 1960s.

The usually highbrow writers H. L. Mencken (later famous as a doyen of American grammar) and George Jean Nathan, who had already published *The Smart Set*, a mixture of gossip and fiction for high society, lost their scruples about the 'lousy' quality and made real money when they began publishing *Saucy Stories* in 1915 and then the *Black Mask*, the most famous in the genre with sales of over 200,000 copies weekly, the exclusive outlet for Carroll John Daly's pioneering private eye Race Williams (avatar of the even harder Dan Turner, star of *Spicy Detective* and *Hollywood Detective Magazine*). Pulp traded in plot-driven thrills and spills, and its division into subgroups made it easy to market. Enduring quality was not an artistic imperative for editors of pulps and the ranks of writers even included gangsters (recruited to write for *True Gang Life*, among other magazines) to add a whiff of notoriety. Nonetheless, the pulps attracted enduring talents such as the detective masters Dashiell Hammett (and his private dicks the Continental-Op in 1923 and later Sam Spade), Raymond Chandler (who invented his first detective Mallory in 1933 and finished off his pulp writing in *Black Mask* with the celebrated Marlowe, a first-person narrator). Other famous names featured in pulps included the great weird story writer H. P. Lovecraft, the science fiction giants Ray Bradbury and Isaac Asimov, and adventure masters Edgar Rice Burroughs and Zane Grey. Even as late as the 1960s the connection between social change and content remained immediate, as can be seen in a gay liberation readership for gay-inflected pulp fiction that boomed in that decade.

Quality periodicals

The view that the short story served as newspaper fodder dogged its reputation from the start. A review in the *Freeman's Journal* of *Tales of the Jury Room* generalized that 'the machinery by which such collections of tales are introduced and connected together is exceedingly cumbersome and uninteresting', deploring the tangled plot. With the publication of stories in *The Yankee* magazine and in other periodicals such as *Burton's Gentleman's Magazine*, of which he was assistant editor, Poe had begun from 1838 to garner a transatlantic reputation for stories appreciated as works of lasting imaginative (and 'morbid') power; they included pioneering criminal fiction as well as more abstract works of symbolist and philosophical thought (many of which made it into his 1840 *Tales of the Grotesque and Arabesque*). Poe's success was more the exception than the rule. In 1857, the critic of *Littel's Living Age*, an American periodical, complained that Poe, while remembered nearly a decade after his death, was still sold as railway reading in cheap portable editions rather than the handsome volumes of a classic. Even conspicuously distinguished literature could be profitably sold cheaply, anticipating the huge rise in pulp magazines after the First World War.

The shift in taste to higher-quality fiction was not immediate, and an oversupply of 'journalized writing' marked by 'sensationalism and crowding of incident' continued to swamp editors through the 1890s and 1900s. In 1881 *Peterson's Magazine*'s editorial 'Chit-Chat' had affirmed its conviction that good fiction was popular fiction. As late as 1891, this ever-popular women's journal boasted that 'no periodical embraces a wider range than ours, comprising first-class fiction' and every 'subject interesting to ladies', which otherwise included pincushions, hardy fuchsias, and earthworms in pots. Its chief excellence was deemed to lie 'in the construction of the story', dismissing great moralists like George Eliot and Thackeray.

Nonetheless, the question of what made a good story was widely asked and a critical backlash against the inferior quality of much fiction grew. The critical and artistic standing of the short story took a favourable turn as writers increasingly perceived its artistic potential. By the turn of the 20th century, literary fiction found outlets in more expensive and overtly elite magazines such as *The Dial*, originally founded in 1840 as a review for philosophy and religion by the New England intellectuals known as the Transcendentalists. The magazine underwent several incarnations as a political and literary review and was re-established as a Modernist journal in the 1920s. In the 1890s, its associate editor, educator and literary critic William Morton Payne, noted appreciatively the variety and quantity of story writing, diversified by region and topic, observing the many contributions to the American tradition of frontier sketches, mountaineer stories, cowboy stories, and army tales. But he also opined that 'the note of distinction (as the French would understand it) is rarely met with in the English or American short story'. Among the quality publications, *Harper's*, a monthly magazine, headed the list and boasted 200,000 subscribers before its demise in 1916. It carved out its niche by serializing English writers like Dickens and Hardy, and from the 1880s began to print American writing, primarily short stories. But it was impossible to restrict the market to literary fiction alone. Too few writers—Payne praised Edith Wharton above all—could fill the gulf between ordinary entertaining stories and the 'pure gold of art'. While O. Henry was appreciated as an American original, magazines repeatedly lambasted writers for being poor imitators of Chekhov and Maupassant, a sign that editors were raising the bar. Amidst the dross, novelists with an established reputation stood the best chance of placing their fictions. Henry James, as his extensive correspondence with publishers like William Dean Howells records, enhanced his income with a steady stream of shorter work.

In Britain, after the First World War the genre of the short story had fallen to a critical low point after the flourishing from around 1880 of Edwardian greats like Hardy, Conrad, and Kipling. Seen by one historian of the form as the mirror to Irish success, the British short story entered what was perceived as a steady decline, although it is an undoubted fact that short fiction continued to enjoy a place in mainstream as well as small press publishing. In praising the fiction of H. G. Wells, one reviewer lamented that magazine editors 'preferred them bad', praising the stories of minor French writers for qualities of 'economy of effect, sincerity and power, that make the average English magazine story seem like the amateur effort of an elderly raconteur after too long a dinner'.

Throughout the 1930s critics complained that the short story in English had become narrow in outlook, writers having caused 'a shrinkage deliberately' by comparison with the novel, contributing to the still entrenched view that the English short story was at a standstill (*Manchester Guardian* 1932) by comparison with the Americans, Irish, and Russians. *The Listener* found the form overexposed and undernourished:

> Gallant warhorses of the form, having sold their eighty stories annually for three decades, sired treatises entitled *The Art of the Short Story*, or for that matter *The Craft of the Short Story*—of which the contents were oddly the same. Young hopefuls took correspondence courses in the justifiable expectation of scratching out a very fair living [see Figure 1].

In 1934 the British weekly the *Observer* ran an article headed 'Is the Short Story Coming Back?', wondering whether signs of improvement had traction. The question posed in that title would be repeated continually for decades to come in British publications.

From the end of the Second World War, the British revival of the short story as a prose genre to be ranked with the novel had its setbacks but also proved lasting. By 1946, V. S. Pritchett, a penetrating critic and short story champion, looked back to the 1920s and saw grounds to revise the standard view of decline. He and other critics revelled in the work of the early Somerset Maugham, Wells, Arnold Bennett, and, above all, Katherine

Mansfield, whose ability to crystallize 'in a cry, a phrase, a gesture, a moment of feeling or vision' captures what was best about the genre that also set it apart from the novel. That appreciation for Mansfield dates back to as early as 1923 when the critic of the *Observer* proclaimed that 'if we rule out elder masters such as Mr. Kipling, the study of the contemporary short story is bound to begin with her name'.

For much of the same period until the 1930s, contemporary critical accounts in America followed a similar history from the doldrums to renaissance. Slice-of-life realism continued to be the dominant trend. Quality outlets such as *Forum* and the *Atlantic Monthly*, the latter founded in 1857 and in the 1870s edited by William Dean Howells, were more exception than rule. By the end of the 1920s, a re-evaluation of the short story canon was under way in America, evidenced by a newfound appreciation for the works of Washington Irving, Hawthorne, and Poe. Their example was invoked in contrast to the great number of periodicals that depended on the 'magnet of brief fiction'.

That the tide had turned convincingly in the United States seemed clear to James Watson, a historian of the American short story, who concludes that 'the short fiction of the thirties is as rich in stories of the first rank as the decade before' when the likes of Hemingway, William Faulkner, Katherine Anne Porter, the young Richard Wright, and very precocious Carson McCullers were in print. In 1940, Dawn Powell, the distinguished New York novelist and diarist, taking the literary temperature, found that 'a book of American stories—covering last 75 years—would be valuable'.

In rejecting the facility that had cheapened standards, the critic Paul Morand wrote in *The Dial* that the successful short story was an 'intellectual sprint that is considered most exhausting'. On the American scene, national pride was increasingly evoked as a factor in new seriousness about the form. This can be seen in a letter to *The Dial* in 1929:

> Since Irving, Poe, and Hawthorne began the cultivation of the fine short narrative among us, the American sense for what should and should not go into a short story seems to have been keener and truer than the English. Kipling and Stevenson are exceptions, but then the one studies Bret Harte, the other Hawthorne.

Foreign influences were also credited positively. A review article in the *Nation* for 1925 ('Short Stories the World Over') has a lot to say about Italian realism in the translation of D. H. Lawrence, the middle-class vulgarity of Thomas Mann's characters, and early Soviet fiction compared to American writers such as O. Henry or Conrad Aiken. Short fiction also scored because it could be timely. The Great Depression elicited social fiction from writers at opposite ends of the political spectrum such as F. Scott Fitzgerald and Theodore Dreiser.

Arguably, it would be the next seventy-five years that saw the short story flourish as never before in both countries, and increasingly in magazines rather than in newspapers. Exceptions to the trend appeared in newspaper outlets with a politicized purpose such as the 'Simple stories' Langston Hughes contributed from 1943 weekly to the *Chicago Defender*, a national African-American newspaper. Magazines enhanced their position as first destination by offering prizes, and publishing annual anthologies of the year's best collection consolidated the impression of a new prestige. Weeklies like *The Nation*, with an emphasis on political news, often carried new works of fiction or articles about literature; cultural magazines like *The Paris Review* (founded 1953) in America and *The Listener* in Britain regularly reviewed books of short stories and most magazines on both sides of the Atlantic advertised regularly for new copy (Figure 4). In Britain, Angus Wilson, a distinguished man of letters, felt as late as the 1960s that magazine serialization still shaped short story collections and anthologies, perhaps more as a commercial fact than a point about the art of the story. In America, the story seemed to be pulling away more overtly from its popular roots.

4. Edwin Muir in *The Listener*, 'There are signs that the story is becoming more popular again.'

The *New Yorker* magazine was founded propitiously in 1925 before the Great Depression in time to capture (and help spearhead) the new wave of interest in short fiction. There is no richer archive of story writing and its indelible contribution to Anglo-American writing, synonymous with a certain type of short story canon—urbane, ironical, and reserved.

To judge from a long essay in *The Nation* ('Keeping the Short Story Alive') the form had once again run into trouble in the 1970s. It was feared that the continued decline of literary periodicals would prove harmful in reducing the opportunities for exposure of younger writers and reduce the appeal of the genre. Yet again a rebound was on the cards. From the 1980s onward there has been a step-change in the modern literary marketplace thanks to the boom of writing workshops and courses, especially in the United States and Britain. Sales of the high-profile yearly anthology *The Best American Short Stories* doubled to 52,000 copies in the five years between 1983 and 1988. The commercial success in this area has not seemingly involved dumbing down.

These anthologies, for example, contain a prefatory essay by important contemporary writers—Joyce Carol Oates and John Updike made notable contributions—that talks about the state of the art and the state of the field and the perennial question of how to pin down the qualities that remain both essential and open to change, valuable indicators of trends in taste. Most interestingly, the anthology ends with a 'Roll of Honor' divided into 'American Authors' and 'Foreign Authors', followed by a list of 'Distinctive Short Stories in American Magazines'. If short story collections rarely top the charts, single author volumes are not a rarity by any means.

In its rich past and ongoing history, the short story has proved agile in exploiting the latest form of dissemination in each media age from newsprint to digital, from novella to flash fiction. Even with variations in length and other features, the longest and most condensed stories tend to exhibit continuities with the traditional structures of beginning, middle, and end, and the love of the twist and reversals. 'Flash fiction tries to tell the biggest, richest, most complex story possible within a certain word limit', a claim to be found on many websites, reminding story lovers that, as in poetry, there is a moment when less becomes more. It remains just the right size for delectation. As if proof were needed that a whole story can fit on a single page, there is the case of the New York bakery that wraps its 'Keret cake' loaf in a short story by the Israeli writer Etgar Keret. Ever malleable and ever focused on the human, the story comfortably straddles the low, middle, and highbrow. During the Covid-19 crisis of 2020 the American author Curtis Sittenfeld published in the *New York Times* a piece called 'Finally Write That Short Story'. She claims that to write a story only requires five steps, and her piece also takes us back to where we started—namely, in a belief that everyone has a story to tell if only they can write it.

Chapter 2
Openings

If there were a contest for the best all-time opening lines of literature, either the Old Testament ('In the beginning God created the heavens and the earth') or the Gospel according to John ('In the beginning was the Word') might well take the prize. Great novels would be just behind. Entire interpretations of Jane Austen's *Pride and Prejudice* and Tolstoy's *Anna Karenina* have pondered whether their plots bear out their respective first lines that 'It is a truth universally acknowledged that a single man in possession of a good fortune must be in want of a wife' and 'All happy families are happy in the same way but an unhappy family is unhappy in its own way.' After these curtain-raisers the novels step back and begin properly.

By contrast, the openings of short stories are already the first act and move swiftly to present subject, event, and motivation, using techniques of speech, viewpoint, description, situation, and timing. Their impact is more pointed on the whole than novelistic openings, as in 'Angela had only one child, a daughter who abhorred her' (Joy Williams, 'Hammer'): like *Anna Karenina*, this start is also about family relations, but concerns one family and one relationship rather than bourgeois families in the abstract. Yet, as Frank O'Connor notes in *The Lonely Voice*, every significant literary story has an initial thesis, covert or declared, that goes beyond the development of plot.

That said, attention-grabbing first lines can provide their own pleasure. Memorable openers are one of the noteworthy features readers have come to expect in genre fiction. Horror stories exploited the framing device that creates out of a social situation, such as a gathering at a club or an after-dinner drink, a chance for one person to recount something uncanny to curious listeners. Numerous classics of the 19th century, from the early E. T. A. Hoffmann's 'The Sandman' to the late R. L. Stevenson's 'The Body-Snatcher', as well as Victorian pieces like Vernon Lee's 'Dionea', Conan Doyle's 'Lot No. 429', and M. P. Shiel's 'Vaila', milk this storytelling aspect. 'I have always maintained, my dear Currier, that if a man wishes to be considered sane, and has any particular regard for his reputation as a truth-teller, he would better keep silent as to the singular experiences that enter his life,' says the hero of John Kendrick Bang's 'Thurlow's Christmas Story' (1894), who luckily for us does not keep silent. Revealing the source of his occult wisdom piques our interest in Robert Howard's 'The Black Stone': 'I read of it first in the strange book of Von Junzt, the German eccentric who lived so curiously and died in such grisly and mysterious fashion. It was my fortune to have access to his *Nameless Cults*.'

Pulp detective stories also have their equivalent opening pattern, normally catching their investigating dicks on the move: 'Inspector Béchoux was in a hurry' (Maurice Leblanc, 'The Arrest of Arsène Lupin'); 'Radford, on his way home one evening, had a fancy to call at the Clover Club to partake of a cocktail' (E. Phillips Oppenheim, 'The Great Bear'). Inevitably, the literary craft of classic detective fiction improved on the devices automatically used in magazine writing, replacing tawdry with snappy, dramatic with cynical. Celebrated detectives like Raymond Chandler's Sam Spade and Samuel Dashiell Hammett's Continental Operative need cases to solve. But they can wait for opportunity to knock: 'I wasn't doing any work that day, just catching up on my foot-dangling' ('Goldfish').

Authors best known outside genre fiction—that is, fiction that 'offers readers more or less what they would expect upon the basis of having read similar books before'—sometimes borrow a leaf from the practices of genre fiction to strike the right tones of horror and existential absurdity. 'I don't know when I died' is how Samuel Beckett launches 'The Calmative'. Few pulp fictions could outdo that for macabre effect. Serious literary fiction can be double-edged about suspense, setting up tension but deflating the whodunit aspect as irrelevant to other aspects of content. D. H. Lawrence's 'The Fox' introduces a vagrant male into the rural habitation of two women, and at the beginning strikes a note of inevitability that looks like a classic spoiler: 'Unfortunately, things did not turn out well.'

Writers like Ray Bradbury (in 'The April Witch' for example), Shirley Jackson, and Stephen King, pioneers in horror and sci-fi, create narrators who are much less self-conscious and mannered than the gentlemanly storytellers. Speakers get right to work in sowing unease: '*Floyd, what's that over there? Oh shit.* The man's voice speaking these words was vaguely familiar, but the words themselves were just a disconnected snippet of dialogue, the kind of thing you heard when you were channel-surfing with the remote.' But O'Connor's rule about a thesis only sometimes looks right. While it suits 'The Fox' and stories that move inexorably to a turning point (when will the fox strike?) and then come full circle (see Chapter 5), there are stories that regress from a starting point and then advance no further. Deborah Eisenberg devised an ingenious temporal structure for 'A Cautionary Tale'. The story begins smack *in medias res* as the characters prepare to board a train and moves forward only to loop back to the beginning just as they enter the station. It has taken the entire space of the story to come full circle, invisibly. Perhaps the title of the story is intended to warn readers about the story itself as much as its plot: namely, not to expect a story to tie everything up neatly.

First impressions

Awareness that closure and resolution have been built into the conception of the story from its start brings an expectation of great economy in plotting and characterization, taking the character briskly up to a turning point and possibly up to but not beyond a new awareness based on an experience. Less usually, cycles of interconnected stories can also take up in stages the resolution of a single predicament such as the gradual decay of a relationship or a family history. The first impression of a character matters critically not only in relation to an endpoint as a measure of whether things have worked out, or a lesson been learned, but also because we wonder whether outcomes are determined by personality or by chance or both. In that respect, the short story, no less than the novel, achieves the illusion of reality by showing characters engaged in making choices, exerting their will, and responding to circumstance based on their own philosophy and interpersonal ability. Stories can have only one opening but they can have more than one introduction.

First impressions in reading stories, rather like meeting people, are an individual and subjective business. In literature and life, how encounters work is open to some generalization more than strict analysis according to rules. The genre has given rise to variation among form-busting writers as well as traditional masters. There might even be debate about where beginnings begin and end. With the title, or the first sentence, or the first page? Paragraphing and changes in narrated speech can be used to demarcate an opening from the body of the story. No fixed rules, however, govern the transition, marked by a change of voice or change of time-frame, from incipit to main story.

Lydia Davis is justly admired for her inventiveness with the short story form. If Munro can push plot and characterization toward the novel, Davis sometimes tests the practice of narrative and definition of structures with microscopic length. Beginning, middle, and end are all seemingly telescoped into a single sentence. 'The Busy Road', which is twenty words held in a single sentence, captures the reaction of the narrator to traffic. While minimalist, it also suggests a back story since the first-person speaker has become accustomed to the noise; and while details of location and time are omitted entirely, the sentence conveys this unknown person's sensitivity when they (gender unknown) remark that the cessation of the noise is disturbing. A single sentence noting a pattern and its disruption contains the past, an event in the present, and an anticipation of the future, and the shape of the story looks like an elaboration of the standard definition of a sentence as subject–verb–object. Its course is impossible to anticipate. There are other stories like 'Almost Over: What's the Word?' that contain more signals. Two people—we presume they are people—met in the past, one remembers the event, and now sums up by commenting on estrangement. The relation of the title to that single utterance puts a spin on a story whose beginning is also, it seems, its end. Beginnings such as these contain enticing and playful effects. But the micro-story or flash fiction is not Davis's primary mode and many of her stories are substantial. Length may not have much bearing on how she achieves aesthetic effects. Her beginnings can be enticing and playful, they can also be true to life by virtue of the situations they create (as in 'The Fish' in which a woman contemplates her propensity for making mistakes while preparing to cook a fish); or funnily absurd (as in 'My Husband and I': 'My husband and I are Siamese twins'); or uncanny and unsettling because pronouns do the grammatical work of being subjects of sentences but are not named or described and minimal subjectivity can be mismatched with their actions ('Her Damage'). In 'Kafka Cooks Dinner' the title makes clear who the 'I' of the first sentence is, corroborated by the mention of 'Milena'. But many stories will predicate universal statements of an 'I', 'she', 'he', and 'we' who remain unnamed.

Who, then, introduces characters to readers? Sometimes it may be the characters themselves. Often, if the intermediary is invisibly subsumed into the prose and the story not told from the viewpoint of anyone in particular, then narration can be assumed to be in the third person. That narrative perspective is assumed to be transparent, and whether the narrator is omniscient and frank or selective with information, or whether the narrator only has partial knowledge, is a matter over which readers might pause to ask questions like, 'How much should be taken on trust?' 'How objective is this?' Classic short stories of the 19th century favoured a third-person narrator in order to create the impression of a window onto life. The strategy cultivates the illusion of knowledge, reaching into the interior of characters as well as seeing their appearance. Yet impersonality may not be entirely what it seems, since third-person viewpoint can offer nuanced judgements.

Inflecting neutral language with minute gradations of opinion is a pervasive fictional technique, bridging omniscience and full subjectivity. (The technique has various names, most commonly 'free indirect speech', and Chekhov was one of its most skilful users.) Hints of bias do not necessarily imply that the narrator is a half-hidden character whose motivation might be revealed. The blended viewpoint, in which the objective third person dominates, enables the author to presume on some common feeling from the reader. In *Dubliners*, one of the great collections whose individual stories rise finally in 'The Dead' to a novelistic complexity of character, Joyce largely filters the personal through the seemingly universal. 'There was no hope for him this time: it was the third stroke' goes the first line in 'The Sisters', the first story in the book. A character's fate is revealed even before 'he' has been described. 'Hope' is what the narrator assumes we all feel for a character in extremis. 'It was the third stroke' delivers the man's fate objectively. But it also emphasizes the helplessness of the victim and his watchers. 'Night after night I had passed the house...' is how the second sentence begins, and the position, age, and status of this speaker in relation to the events inside the house gradually come together over the course of the story. The narrator's restrained tone in the description of intimate scenes, sometimes scenes of depravity and squalor, avoids sensationalism and even strikes a note of sympathy.

The third-person narrator remains hard to beat as a default mode. Confidence in the reliability and disinterest of third-person omniscient narrators—Tolstoy and Turgenev are often cited as best practitioners—continues in a fine tradition of latter-day realists, including names such as William Trevor, Yiun Li, Anita Desai, and Ruth Prawer Jhabvala, whose works often (though not always) allow readers to accept statements about characters as true. Postmodernist writing had a field day undermining omniscience, nowhere better seen than in the stories of Robert Coover and Donald Barthelme, masters of metafiction who love to reveal the narrative scaffolding for the contrivance it is. In recent years, post-postmodernist short story writing in many countries seems to have relaxed back into a less ironic and self-reflective concern with the story as its own subject. But one legacy of the current version of realism may be a move away from plain third-person narration. Lorrie Moore likes to mix up voices by splicing snippets of external viewpoint into the stream of conversation, pushing the narrator onto the same level as characters. Even bodies talk in her stories: 'The grumblings of their stomachs were intertwined and unassignable. "Was that you or was that me?" she would ask in bed, and Dench would say, "I'm not sure."' ('Wings') In fact, Dench, reminiscent of Densher, the hero of Henry James's *Wings of the Dove*, puts his finger on something else, something more general about the short story. Being 'not sure' is a state of mind that the short story excels in revealing, and the genre is comfortable with leaving readers uncertain about characters as well as depicting uncertainty felt by characters themselves.

Viewpoint can be multifaceted. Consider another type of third-person narrator, one whose knowledge of characters really makes them first-person speakers in disguise. Saul Bellow's speaker in 'The Old System' exhibits a remarkable knowledge of his subject, Dr Braun, starting from the bottom up ('He dried himself with yesterday's shirt, an economy') and ending with: 'It was a thoughtful day for Dr Braun.' So close is the narrator to Dr Braun, a psychiatrist, that we might wonder whether in fact Dr Braun and the narrator are actually one and the same. Has Bellow split Dr Braun, a psychiatrist, into the voice of the narrating superego and Dr Braun the object of his attention? That would be an artful twist on the usual role of each vantage point. Full-fledged first-person narrators would seem to promise authentic psychological exploration of character. Who better than the 'I' to explain states of mind and actions set out either as an oral monologue or in the form of a story written as a memoir or diary?

In practice, 'I-narrators' tend to be larger-than-life personalities who revel in performative display, spilling their guts or playing mind-games with themselves (and the reader) or simply talking aloud. They can also be accomplished dissemblers. Henry James's *The Turn of the Screw* begins in that familiar manner of the third-person frame ('The story had held us, round the fire, sufficiently breathless...'), and shifts into the voice of an 'I-narrator' whose latent hostility gives the psychological twist to the story. Not all of these figures need to take themselves too seriously, however. Etgar Keret's stories are barely more than anecdotes with a single plot line and closer to stand-up. His opening lines have that sort of improvisational feel: 'I talk too much' ('Upgrade'), to which the reader might say 'Who am I to disagree?'; 'There are conversations that can change a person's life. I'm sure of it. I mean, I'd like to believe it' ('Joseph'), about which the reader might say, 'Are you sure? Really?' The illusion of immediate interaction with the speaker is the hook that draws us in. These wise guys are not very distant cousins to the unstoppable monologists, who speak directly to the reader and plumb the depths aloud.

'I am a sick man…I am a nasty man. An unattractive man am I,' says the unnamed hero of Dostoevsky's *Notes from the Underground*, a long short story that is a landmark in ego-narration, a classic work of urban alienation and portrait of the neurotic. Its brilliance as a story lies in the illusion that somehow the way into the irrational self, the pure id that lies at the bottom of personality, is through constant self-consciousness that requires a listener who cannot talk back. Heirs to Dostoevsky's monologist include Woody Allen's story 'Notes from the Overfed' ('I am fat. I am disgustingly fat. I am the fattest human I know'), whose narrator's riff is on the morality and metaphysics of fat—the substance itself, the bourgeois morality of fat, its advantages and disadvantages. The opening salvo of David Foster Wallace's 'Good Old Neon' bypasses Allen to revive the example of the Russian master: 'My whole life I've been a fraud. I'm not exaggerating. Pretty much all I've ever done all the time is try to create a certain impression of me in other people.' Sustaining that impression over the course of the story is a matter of doing the voices, techniques discussed in Chapter 3.

First-person is the natural mode for retrospective stories that explore the past. Stories written this way look to the past for a formative emotional truth. Often the act of recounting conflates past and present as characters relive what they felt at the time. Very much in this retrospective vein of analysis and nostalgia are stories such as 'Doorways' by John McGahern and 'Communist' by Richard Ford. Each of these retrospective stories begins with a sympathetic musing aloud, spoken perhaps more to the self than to a stranger. 'There are times when we see the small events we look forward to…', says McGahern's narrator, uttering a universal about how we live life forward but understand by looking back. The past may be as distant as a moment ago. A day in the life of a teenager, now remembered for not clarifying his state of confusion, constitutes the action of Ford's story as narrated by the older hero:

> My mother once had a boyfriend named Glen Baxter. This was in 1961. We—my mother and I—were living in the little house my father had left her up the Sun River, near Victory, Montana, west of Great Falls. My mother was thirty-one at the time. I was sixteen. Glen Baxter was somewhere in the middle, between us, though I cannot be exact about it.

Memory is a mixture of precision (the year, the names, the places, the age), helping to effect closure on an episode, and the impressionistic by delicately hinting at an element of sexual rivalry between the adolescent boy and his mother's boyfriend complicated by his own need, perhaps hinted at here, for a substitute father figure.

First-person stories are by no means the retreat of Dostoevskyan solipsists. In Ann Beattie's collection *The Burning House*, the narrator continually tries to batten down her own identity while being aware of the fluidity she sees in the behaviour of others: 'Freddy Fox is in the kitchen with me. He has just washed and dried an avocado seed I don't want, and he is leaning against the wall, rolling a joint. In five minutes, I will not be able to count on him' ('The Burning House'). The narrator remains at ease describing the states in which characters find themselves ('more comfortable', 'feeling affectionate', 'so lucky') but the observation that 'I have known everybody in the house for years, and as time goes by I know them all less and less' bears out Margaret Atwood's view of that collection as a bulletin on 'what's happening out there on the edge of that shifting and dubious no man's land known as interpersonal relations'.

Lasting impressions

Novels can give the impression of omniscience and open-endedness. In the short story, knowledge is understood to be limited by time and perspective. Plots might last long enough to get to the heart of a personality. Information about characters is on a need-to-know basis, meaning just enough of the salient personality traits and physical features, inevitably short of a complete picture, is revealed. Part of the writer's assumed contract with the reader is that we piece together what we can't know. This phenomenon is something Eudora Welty recognizes in her essay 'Looking at Short Stories' in which, putting some justifiable vagueness into the equation, she speaks of how stories operate according to first impressions rather than fixed logic. Readers are sometimes allowed to know characters better than they know themselves, or to participate in the confusion.

Katherine Mansfield's stories regularly begin *in medias res* with people and events in unsettled states—characters in motion, on thresholds, evading routine, or finding that it evades them. Vagueness about location captures the state of muddle out of which her characters never quite manage to talk themselves, despite an amusing loquacity. In 'The Garden Party', one of her most famous works, well-laid plans teeter on the brink of disaster—the recognition that 'after all the weather was ideal' is no reassurance. In 'Marriage à la Mode' (1921), a family is thrown into bohemian tumult by the wife's love life that keeps a thwarted husband in uncertainty ('On his way to the station William remembered with a fresh pang of disappointment that he was taking nothing down to the kiddies'), an opening that suggests that this is a story about the inattention that causes people to stray. In 'Bains Turcs', a terse opening instruction ('"Third storey—to the left, Madame," said the cashier') gets a young woman more than she bargained for in a public bathhouse when some odd strangers stripped naked lay bare their feelings. All characterization is necessarily incomplete, but there are cases when the reader's insights cannot exceed the characters' own blinkered self-knowledge.

Yet short stories can also endeavour to extract from a whole life an episode that telescopes a cross-section of past, present, and future. Even in his shorter fiction Thomas Mann looks like the consummate 19th-century novelist because he is able to provide ample back-story for a character before resuming in the fictional present. A writer of naturalistic precision, with an ear for the social nuance of the English and Irish middle classes, William Trevor can scale down an entire life to the aftermath of a childhood incident carefully told, or to a late chapter after a lifetime of routine. He is also an elegiac writer and conveys how the repetition of ritual blunts an awareness of time passing. His characters measure the span of their lives through a yearly routine that sets their social clock.

In 'Afternoon Dancing', the lives of individuals look fully realized when set within the history of their friendship. Two middle-aged couples, Alice and Lenny, and Poppy and Albert, have returned 'every summer since the war' to the Prospect Hotel to dance (note the name of the venue: the story will be about new marital chances). The third-person narrator takes a more objective view by noting the year when each pair married (1938) and the year in which their children marry and, in one case, emigrate to Canada (1969). Much of the descriptive information could have been rendered as dates only. Would anyone miss the names of children we never meet again or the street addresses? Incidental detail and specific years vouchsafe realism. But from the start character portrayal is built on a substructure of sameness and repetition. The words 'all' and 'same' recur: 'same schools', 'same street', 'all married', 'all in their mid-fifties', 'all run to fat', and friendship is built on a litany of common practices, class, and even body shape. Routine puts the life of the friendship on a schedule defined by rhythms that absorbs the shocks of economic and social change. A bereavement occurs. The question for the couples is: what challenge does finding a new dance partner on the floor, and possibly in life, represent?

Writers such as William Trevor, Gabriel García Márquez, and Alice Munro create worlds in a short compass. Stories that in paraphrase might seem to have a linear plot acquire depth from their connectedness to anterior and concurrent stories that can invisibly shape the direction a life takes. Munro's 'Hateship, Friendship, Courtship, Loveship, Marriage' takes up the experience of an immigrant woman, Johanna Parry, who is determined to establish her own home. She reveals in a letter to Ken, the man she decides to marry and the former son-in-law of her employer, that she arrived in Canada as a young girl on 'a Plan'. Relentlessly gruff and not one 'to charm or entice', she has no gift for any of the '-ships' used and coined in Munro's title. A housekeeper and professional companion, she enjoyed the esteem of a Mrs Willets who left her a legacy on her death and goes about her job unassumingly in service to Mr McAuley. The chronological structure of the story is used to underscore Johanna's impression of life as something that will fall in place if she wills it: the furniture she appropriates implies a home, a home implies a husband, and that requires marriage. She remains impervious to the hatreds, friends, courting, and love that define most marriage plots and still succeeds. But the story itself undermines her belief that she stands alone because other people with all the feelings she lacks such as hatred, friendship, and romance accidentally produce the outcome she desired. A line from Virgil's *Aeneid* appears at the end in a piece of Latin schoolwork, and it is the Sibyl of Cumae's advice not to ask what fate has in store. If this is not a story primarily about ironic reversal it is possibly because the knowledge of what fate has in store for her means nothing to Johanna.

It is obvious why in the case of some modes, such as genre fiction, formulaic structures work best. If the plot entails exploding a bomb, a fuse needs to be lit early, and the same principle applies outside genre fiction to most stories whose effect of suspense and rescue is central (something we shall see in the case of George Saunders's 'Victory Lap', discussed later). While there is no lack of clear formulas for how to open a story, great short stories elude the foursquare shape of a scheme. Katherine Mansfield, always an innovator in the form, dispensed with introductions as obstacles.

Johanna Parry dreams of destinations, well aware how circuitous life can be. That seems part and parcel with the emphasis of Munro's opening words, which fall first on her as she considers travel along the 'many branch lines', followed by her description as a 'woman with a high, freckled forehead and frizz of reddish hair'. Munro's gift in creating characters with an autonomous life was not restricted to separate stories. The sequence of related stories about a mother and daughter in *The Beggar Maid* has a novelistic scope. 'Hateship, Friendship, Courtship, Loveship, Marriage' is not the beginning of a sequence; it is a self-contained story with no unfinished business. Would there be any point in elaborating future chapters in Johanna's life? Her personality is unified to such a degree that one episode suffices to capture what she has always done and will always do—that is, meet the challenges life throws her way until she can make a home. The lasting impression of characters definitively conditioned by their state of being—widowhood in the case of 'Afternoon Dancing', migration in Johanna's—unfolds organically from first impressions.

Chapter 3
Voices

What would short stories be without voices? The genre is the perfect platform for self-engrossed characters whose egotism is more bearable in shorter doses than for entire novels. Voices can come at you with straightforward appeals, or advice, like the speaker in Alice Munro's 'Pride', whose opening line is 'Some people get everything wrong? How can I explain?' They can come at you from unexpected places, such as the hero of V. S. Pritchett's 'The Oedipus Complex', whose comic monologue is delivered from the dentist's chair, reducing him frequently to 'bla bla', the sort of gag that could never make a novel. Or they can emanate spookily from the afterlife in fictions inspired by horror and ghost stories such as García Márquez's 'The Other Side of Death' and Dostoevsky's 'Bobok'. Sometimes voices jump off the page when a story contains an embedded message (letter, telegram, tweet) as in James Baldwin's 'Sonny's Blues', sometimes they are deadpan, a frequent style in Helen Garner's stories ('My friend is tone deaf', 'The Life of Art'), and sometimes, as in Jamaica Kincaid's sassy 'Girl', there is no way of knowing where a stream of consciousness riffing to oneself about how to behave will lead.

In English fiction from the Romantic period to the Edwardians the use of a performative frame was a popular device and made the voice and personality of the primary narrator a key source of variation. Writers such as Sir Walter Scott, Kipling, Edith Wharton, and above all the great Russians, such as Ivan Turgenev and Nikolai Leskov, often structure their works as tales generated by a chance encounter. Stories arise from situations in which travellers or fellow guests bide their time at an inn or after a dinner in front of a cosy fire. A first-person narrative can repel, invite confidence, lie subtly or extravagantly. Voices do not just deliver content. Monologues and dialogues are soundscapes as well as content; they convey linguistic usage of voices inflected for class, ethnicity, and generation. Reading between the lines, we try to hear other intentions in the narrator's recital. As Amy Hempel put it, the story 'engages with ordinary people, ordinary matters, recognizable stuff. But this is all a masquerade.'

Where does the voice come from?

Searching for true identity behind the projected persona, Eudora Welty said she was always 'listening for a story'. Few practitioners can better Welty in using dialogue to create an instant impression of the chattiness of small-town Southern life. And few subsequent American writers possess a keener ear than Edward P. Jones for speech and regional dialect. His mastery in creating characters through voice also de-centres plots and relaxes the shape of stories. A Jones story is about the layered experience of first- and second-generation descendants of slaves who migrated from the south to Washington, DC. Their urban experience is mapped precisely on the city grid, but narrative often strays from the main plot without explanatory signals. Jones's stories usually do circle back to their principal subject, but not before characters open the narrative up to the histories of older relatives or the current kinship group. Hence a main voice can spool out into the collateral stories of secondary and minor characters that hang like branches off the main narrative trunk. In a story like 'In a Blink of God's Eye', the structure and mythic manner seem so expansive and digressive they can even recall the technique of a writer like

García Márquez. Out of a multitude of contrasting types of speech, dialectical and educated, also come generational contrasts in the use of folkloric motifs, rationalist outlooks, and racial attitudes.

Short stories can probe the inner worlds of characters with no less insight and focus than the novel. Sometimes the entirety of a story may coincide with that focus on subjectivity. One way into the essential self, if such a thing is conceivable, is by letting a protagonist pour it all out. The nervous and voluble speakers of Jean Rhys's first-person stories, nowhere better experienced than in 'Vienne', are alcohol-fuelled monologists. Few literary characters spill the beans as memorably as the hero of Dostoevsky's *Notes from the Underground*. Part One consists entirely of an energetic monologue that rails against prevailing social ideologies, like rationalism and utilitarianism. Few literary characters could have greater cause for complaint than the hero of Lev Tolstoy's story 'Kholstomer', a talking horse on his last legs who is also naively voluble and, like Tolstoy's human heroes, too involved in life to see death around the corner. Both masterpieces, written at a period when the Realist novel dominated, dispense with the third-person omniscient narrator crucial to the 'reality effect', privileging instead accesses of attention and haphazard observation the subject talks about to the reader.

Dorothea Brande, in her classic *Becoming a Writer* (1934), repeatedly observes that the sort of person who likes to examine her dreams, to record personal moments of intensity, is probably a short story writer. That was a sound conclusion to reach twenty years after the publication of Joyce's *Dubliners*, a landmark book of stories that synthesize an entire human and urban landscape out of human dramas individually and perfectly realized. Like all the stories in *Dubliners*, 'Eveline' is a master class in character portraiture achieved through subtle inflections of narrative voice and the interchange of first- and third-person voices. The emotional work of the story comes in the subtle interrelation between the heroine's interior voice and that of the narrator who knows her better than she knows herself, albeit only incompletely and from a partial point of view. In a story that culminates in an act of not saying, Joyce's narrator is the one character who resembles the heroine in avoiding outbursts. Eveline is portrayed in a moment of introspection, pondering separation from her home and reminded of other people who had come and gone in her life either by travelling away or dying. It is only after several pages that the reader learns that she is 'about to explore another life with Frank', who promises to take her by the 'night-boat to be his wife and to live with him in Buenos Ayres [*sic*] where he had a home waiting for her'. When an unexpected backlash occurs, the drama of her doubt about the courtship is all the more shocking for the violence it does to the quiet interiority established in the story from the opening page. Tormented by the possibility of eloping abroad, the heroine guards her secret from her family and keeps her doubts from her fiancé. She yearns for freedom from the constraints of life and the state of mental subjugation that is her real prison.

At the opening, she sits at the window watching the world go past (a common posture for women represented in short stories). The real window is the narrator's insight into her feelings. Inner and outer worlds have the same air of distance and neutrality. Here the boundary between Eveline's thoughts and the narrator's voice is entirely permeable, and there is scarcely a sentence in the narrator's use of the third person and free indirect discourse that the reader cannot convert into first-person utterance by changing pronouns yet for no gain (or loss) of intimacy: 'My father was not so bad then' is no more intensely confessional than 'Her father was not so bad then', and it is open to question whether 'Now I am going to go away like the others, to leave my home' is obviously more poignant than Joyce's actual 'Now she was going to go away like the others, to leave home.'

The longer Eveline contemplates her decision, the more her thoughts encompass the judgements of others as she imagines what people will say when they learn of her elopement, or, as she imagines her colleagues in the shop will put it more tartly, that she has 'run away with a fellow'. As paragraphs go by, Joyce shifts away from this transparent neutrality toward a tension between self-knowledge and speculation. Knitted together in the third-person prose are sentences inflected more emphatically with Eveline's voice and other sentences emanating from an outside perspective. What would marriage do for her? 'People would treat her with respect then', an assertion that Eveline makes to herself, could be spoken in the third-person.

By contrast, the meaning of another phrase ('she sometimes felt herself in danger of her father's violence') would not be the same if it were rewritten in Eveline's voice, which might sound like 'I sometimes feel that father will beat me.' Her more direct utterances belong to the world in which she has always lived. What her present life means to her in terms of domestic routine is interpreted by phrases that come more naturally to the narrator and convey a greater distance than Eveline could achieve: 'invariable squabble for money', 'elbowed her way through the crowds', 'under her load of provisions'. Eveline's imagination moves paratactically through the juxtaposition of concrete scenes. When she thinks of Frank, it is of 'his peaked cap pushed back on his head and his hair tumbled forward over a face of bronze'. The narrative style allows her to define her own character by measuring out information with great precision: she tells us that he 'used to call her Poppens out of fun', that he 'started as a deck boy at a pound a month on a ship of the Allan Line', that he 'had sailed through the Straits of Magellan'. To whom does the summarizing phrase 'tales of distant countries' belong? Is that the phrase of a father who prevents her courtship because, as he is quoted saying, 'I know these sailor chaps'? Could the phrase be Eveline's? It is the narrator's job to capture her romantic longing as an opposition between the prosaic and the exotic; and to qualify it subtly so that the reader perceives how alien a phrase like 'tales of distant countries' would be to a character like

Eveline, whose awareness in the very opening of the story is of 'the odour of dusty cretonne', who can hear 'footsteps clanking along the concrete pavement' and 'afterwards crunching on the cinder path'.

Such an accumulation of detail, auditory, visual (houses are 'brown' and 'bright brick' and 'red'), and social (all the people mentioned have names) is not only or merely about the solidity of realism. Its effect is psychological, since the more Eveline struggles to tear herself away, the more tangible the world becomes to her. As the moment for her departure approaches it is that 'odour of dusty cretonne' that triggers an involuntary memory of a pledge she gave her mother: 'She knew the air. Strange that it should come that very night to remind her of the promise to her mother, her promise to keep the home together as long as she could.' Joyce's control of nuance is such that a single word conveys a tremor of doubt. Between the opening page, with its first mention of dust, and this second mention a few pages later, probably only a few minutes have elapsed, during which an entire family history has been encapsulated. The intensification of noticing belies the wish to depart. 'Strange' is the word Eveline gives to a sense of dread she cannot quite recognize. It makes out of a commonplace smell something like an omen. Her mother's remembered speech bursts into her head in the repeated Irish Gaelic phrase: 'Derevaun Seraun! Derevaun Seraun!' meaning 'At the end of pleasure, there is pain.' And the phrase breaking into her consciousness provokes a 'sudden impulse of terror' and resolution to escape.

Without transition the story moves abruptly to its next location at the station and the quay. It is for the narrator to express what Eveline now feels ('a maze of distress') and to solidify her instinctive terror of escape in the image of the boat as a 'black mass'. Like 'a helpless animal', as the narrator says, she senses that the real meaning of her terror lies not in a fear of not escaping but in her inability to leave. Earlier footsteps clacked on the pavement, now 'a bell clanged upon her heart' and her heart opens to a fear of that black mass. Is she afraid of drowning? Or does she have an inkling, as has been argued, that she will be a victim of the white slave trade and sold on when they reach Argentina? What hangs in the balance in the final moment is the choice between departure and parting, and it is tipped toward staying by terror at the unknown. In her own mind she is already drowning even though she is rooted to the quay: 'Her hands clutched the iron [railing] in frenzy. Amid the seas she sent a cry of anguish.' Frank's cries 'Come!' intensify the drama. Father, mother, and lover all speak, but Eveline in the course of the entire story is not heard aloud. Her protest is entirely to herself ('No! No! No! It was impossible'), her silence rebuffing his cry of 'Eveline! Evvy!' The entire fantasy of romantic escape ends with 'no sign of love or farewell or recognition'. Monologues can be solemn or ebullient, as outrageous as stand-up—or nearly as voicelessly interior as a painting.

Social comedy of courtship

There are few situations in which the way people speak and listen and the way silences can be left hanging matter more than in courtship. Courtship has the further advantage, as material for the short story, that it compresses cause and effect into near simultaneous action, a key element in the success of the genre. Dialogue can take us straight into the unvarnished portrayal of lovers as they choose to play their parts. Few stories are written purely in dialogue, and in stories in which dialogue dominates the role of the narrator may be more partial than detached, coming close to the viewpoint of one of the characters. This mixed form, a technique perfected by Chekhov, is what we find in Richard Yates's 'The Best of Everything'. First published in 1952 and often anthologized, the story is a social comedy about the impending wedding of the clever Grace. Nothing like Joyce's Eveline, Grace is a career girl (in the period idiom), more forceful and better educated, who has the upper hand over her working-class boyfriend Ralph. A period milieu, marked by dictaphones and central typing pools, today scarcely recognizable tools of the then-modern office, provided fertile ground for realist art in the period. Unobtrusive details speak volumes about expectation. Grace, who wants the best of everything, looks forward to wedding gifts from Bloomingdales, the high-end department store that stands for Manhattan sophistication, whereas Ralph hails from working-class Queens.

Such details are as much of the cityscape as the reader gets. Yates builds most scenes out of conversations, individual styles of speech always indicative of background and personality. Writers of the modern short story splice spoken exchanges into narrative, sometimes to add a casual element of misdirection. Characters in dialogue also perform to one another, raising questions about the authenticity and sincerity inherent in social life and regular acts of communication. How they talk to one another, and how (and even whether) they hear and listen to one another can approximate the technique of stage play or film script through the clever use of the narrator. Yates's narrator is split between the scene-setting function of a director who structures action and provides stage directions (details of interiors, dress, transportation, and drink) and the gossipy function of a friend who dispenses commentary with a deadpan irony.

Irony is the consistent feature in how characters speak to one another because most conversations are somewhat off-beam as characters talk past one another. While 'crazy' about one another, the lovebirds find it hard to speak. Yates solves the problem of how to preserve that awkwardness and move the story forward by engaging a third person to comment on the relationship and provide back-story. Either Grace or Ralph features in each conversation with a third character, and Yates maintains the balance of contrast and similarity between the two by choosing for each the same set of respective interlocutors: a colleague, a best friend or roommate, and finally one another.

This is a way of maintaining discretion about past indiscretions. 'Mr Atwood [Grace's boss] had treated her with a special courtliness ever since the time she necked with him at the office Christmas party.' When they are briefly alone together once again, Atwood pins a white corsage to her dress, like a badge of restored innocence. In their brief chat, Grace plays at role reversal, arguing that her boss should not spare her workload just because of her engagement, while Atwood protests, 'You only get married once.' Grace by name, grace by gesture, virtue is restored. No sooner has Grace finished with her boss than Ralph rings her at work to say that his boss has given him a fifty-dollar bonus. Grace's colleagues have just admired a snapshot of Ralph ('Oh, he's so *cute!*') but we hear him before we see him: 'How ya doin', honey?' Throughout, Grace's language will be genteel. She first uses 'lovely', a favourite adjective in this conversation to which Ralph responds, '"Lovely, huh?" he said with a laugh, mocking the girlishness of the word. "Ya *like* that, huh, Gracie?"' All of Ralph's speech effects will be resolutely oral and working-class, recognizable to readers of Damon Runyon, whose characters embodied New York speech full of 'siz' for 'says', 'ya' for 'you', 'honey' to Grace's 'darling', and relentlessly in the Runyonesque present tense. Martha, Grace's roommate, has the classic role of the sidekick and comic foil. We first hear her critically mimicking Ralph's accent: 'Isn't he funny?' Martha had said after their first date. 'He says "terlet." I didn't know people really said "terlet [toilet]."' In two pages, Yates telescopes their relationship by summarizing the first debriefing they had after Grace met Ralph, taking it up to the present as Martha tries one last time to dissuade Grace from marrying a man she regards as uncouth.

While the narrator's conclusions are laden with irony, Martha's job as foil is to offset Grace's more nuanced judgement and tone down Ralph's hearty sentiments for whom she is an equal match. He remains resolutely deaf to the social nuance of situation, and his girlfriend's tone becomes increasingly wisecracking in response to his obliviousness. Part of the social comedy lies in how the story's structure creates echoes. Grace and her roommate Martha are just as prone to miscommunication as Grace and Ralph. While inwardly troubled by Martha's attitude and dislike of Ralph, Grace outwardly pretends to shrug off her concerns and is as mulish to Martha as Ralph is to her. Eventually Martha repents of her criticism and then confides that she's going on a trip a day early in order to let Grace spend the evening on her own with Ralph and show off from her trousseau the sheer white negligée her girlfriends have given her. As Grace contemplates seducing Ralph, the story cuts to Ralph and his friend Eddie. Their banter moves from barstools to a luggage store (a gift of a suitcase) to the bachelor party, and the entire sequence is almost rendered as snippets of banter, songs ('Fa he's a jolly guh fella'). Calls for Ralph to give a speech fail as he is overcome with emotion, proof that he is happiest talking with rather than talking to. Grace, however, much prefers talking at. He may literally have the last word when he wishes Grace goodnight—she, however, unthinkingly closes the door on him. The abiding impression at the end is of a couple who will talk volubly at cross-purposes. The success of their marriage might lie in their obliviousness to what each is saying.

How voice is used can be a key difference in stories about similar material. Silent understanding cuts through the courtship plot of Bernard Malamud's 'The Magic Barrel'. Like the stories by Joyce and Yates, it is a story of romance. The principal voice belongs to a marriage broker who aims to manipulate his client into marrying his daughter. The magic barrel is the metaphorical term given by the rabbinical student Leo Finkle to the source from which the marriage broker Pinye Salzman produces card files of eligible brides for his reluctant client. Malamud's representation of the world often hovers between the real and the fantastic, and this story similarly keeps one foot in the folkloric or fantastic and another in the recognizable landscape of New York. Certain mannerisms of speech and insight belonging to the narrator blur the boundary, starting from the qualifications and slight contradictions of the opening sentence: 'Not long ago there lived in uptown New York, in a small, almost meager room, though crowded with books, Leo Finkle, a rabbinical student in the Yeshivah University.' The temporal and the spatial are equally pseudo-precise, with 'not long ago' having the same effect as 'once upon a time'. Leo has been at his studies for six years, but events unfolding from his meeting Salzman take up 'one night'. Throughout the story, the narrator subsumes into his speech whole phrases that must belong to Finkle ('for six years he devoted himself entirely to his studies'; 'Therefore he thought it the better part of trial and error—of embarrassing fumbling—to call in an experienced person to advise him in these matters'). Salzman, by contrast, speaks for himself in a Yiddish-inflected patois: 'On this girl, God bless her, years are not wanted. Each one that it comes makes better the bargain'; or 'A sliced tomato you have maybe?'

Three encounters make up the heart of the story: the first interview between client and marriage broker; a meeting between Leo and Lily Hirschorn, one of the eligible women whose questions about piety provoke Leo to re-examine his faith; and a final interview with Salzman in which Leo compels him to arrange a meeting with the one woman whose photo captivates him obsessively. The speech patterns of each character remain vividly intact. Yet it is impossible not to notice an odd feature of the narrator's own style. His speech is strongly demarcated by the heavy use of adverbs especially when setting up dialogue between other characters. Adverbs not only control how readers hear the dialogue; they also mark the tendency of a narrator determined that we hear everything as spoken 'bravely', 'frankly', 'gravely', 'harshly', 'courteously'; and thoughts are realized 'gradually', 'seriously', 'truly' and not only 'deeply' but also 'seen in the depths of eyes'.

However, the narrator's position may not be any more privileged than the reader's. While Salzman spreads photos on the table, Leo stares out the window: 'he observed the round white moon, moving high in the sky through a cloud-menagerie, and watched with half-open mouth as it penetrated a huge hen and dropped out of her like an egg laying itself.' Not even Salzman could guess the semi-erotic nature of Leo's imagination as it occurs here. The egg is a Kabbalistic symbol of the wholeness of God, but also patently erotic. Leo might speak 'gravely', 'harshly', and 'softly', but a latent romanticism pushes him toward the one woman Salzman tries to keep from him ('She is a wild one—wild without shame. This is not a bride for a rabbi'). She is Stella, Salzman's own daughter, and Leo arranges an assignation described in the final scene. 'Violins and lit candles revolved in the sky.' In a story full of banter, theirs is the only encounter that passes as wordless, a pantomime of gestures with Leo thrusting flowers, Stella smoking, her eyes full of 'desperate innocence', and Salzman chanting 'prayers for the dead', possibly because in making a match he has guaranteed Leo's loss of innocence. How to render speechlessness as its own powerful message is a problem that Malamud solves brilliantly by juxtaposing Salzman's endless talk and the couple's silence: a duality of empty voices and silent connection.

Dialogue as distance

The use of dialogue in the short story has not been a constant feature. Conversation in snatches was a regular feature of unskilled writing at the height of the magazine period. Subsequently discouraged by many style manuals, dialogue has again become essential shorthand in creating effects of characterization, realism, and regional inflection. Later practitioners of the literary story are skilled inventors and stenographers of speech effects and intonations to convey characters' social origins, race and ethnicity, class, and education. We have already seen in 'The Best of Everything' how dialogue can short-circuit elaborate plots. Conversation can cut straight to the chase, efficiently delivering plot through personal voice and viewpoint. Yet short story dialogue often provides illustrations of frustrated communication. By leaving the reader to witness misunderstandings and failures in self-understanding, the short story can convey with maximum brevity the illusion of psychological depth and the awkwardness of intimate encounters. Tragedies of misunderstanding pervade the form, nowhere better than in stories of love gained and lost; and there are comedies of non-communication that can only be sustained for the length of a short story, for instance in writers like Samuel Beckett and Muriel Spark, whose characters reel off their pet peeves, oblivious to the other speaker.

In Lorrie Moore's 'Two Boys', postcards and phones are the means of communication between Mary, a mentally fragile heroine, and the two boyfriends of the title who, otherwise nameless, remain known as Number One and Number Two (the first is a politician campaigning for office who boasts of being number one on a poster). Her name, however, might be part of a set of oblique biblical references and images, in this case suggesting a link with Mary Magdalene. Moore's Mary daily steps through gutters of blood from the slaughterhouse above which she lives ('Pork blood limned their shoes'); she regularly obsesses over purity, bathing in Lysol, and even dresses all in white, head to toe. She reads biblical poetry while sitting in the local park where an odd little girl, also unnamed and like some precocious double ('I'm waiting for my boyfriends'), meets her three times, professes to have a 'message from outer space', spits at her, and in the final pages pronounces surreally that 'they are all dead'. The narrator comments that 'it was way too warm for fall' and it is hard not to think of a biblical fall as the little girl and Mary, who repeatedly clutches her stomach, stare 'at the meat displayed in the windows, the phallic harangue of sausages, marbled, desiccated, strung up as for a carnival'. That fall from abstinence or at least fidelity into guilt and guilt-ridden symbolism is the distance travelled from the opening paragraph. She has bought a postcard of an Annunciation, the 'peacock-handsome angel holding up fingers and whispering, *One boy, two boys*', and her text on the back of a postcard provides a first sample of a cast of mind oscillating between the high-flown and the earthy: 'Unveil thyself! Unblacken those teeth and minds! Get more boys in your life!'

Two boys presuppose two voices, which in the first half of the story are both spliced into a descriptive pattern moving in and out of Mary's head and observing the world as presented by the narrator. Her interaction with the two men is like some sort of emotional pinball as she shuffles between them depending on their availability. A married man, Number One is sarcastic, unreliable (his children provide a convenient excuse leading to the terse rejection on the phone, 'I may not be able to see you, Mary'), and relatively chatty. 'He was the funny one. After they made love, he'd sigh, open his eyes, and say, "Was that you?"' Number Two is tactile but taciturn ('not so hilarious') and barely able to articulate his feelings. Snippets of dialogue are used for declarations that sound unfelt and mere performance: '"I love you," Mary said to Number One', which elicits '"You're very special, too," he replied. And "I love you," she said to Number Two.' He replies, sputtering in a choked voice, '"I love you, too."' Each pair of statements is printed at the left of the page almost like a set of rhymes: the reiteration and asymmetric responses, ending with 'too', suggest a situation equivalent to an off rhyme, that is, a situation that is off-kilter. Page layout proves a useful device, and is once again skilfully used at the end of a paragraph beginning with postcards from the two friends. Their comments to Mary include the teasing admonition 'You hog', a reminder perhaps of the pork blood (and perhaps the swine that, like biblical demons, have to be cast off from this now impure Mary?), and are then rounded off with the comments each friend sent on seeing her redecorated flat. Number One remains self-aware and aware of appearances whereas Number Two only has eyes for her.

> 'You've redecorated,' said Number One.
>
> 'Do you really love me?' said Number Two. He never looked around. He stepped toward her, slowly, wanting to know only this.

No answer is forthcoming. After Mary returns from a trip to Canada the story's soundscape becomes increasingly bizarre. Spurious voices emanating from a tape-recorder and the telephone intrude fragmentary remarks. Conversations between Mary and her boyfriends are no longer fully reported as the relationships become more attenuated, leaving only non sequiturs suspended on the page with no explicit context. Again, Moore uses lineation to brilliant effect in moving from one disconnected exchange to another:

> 'Charity that crude dehumanizes,' said Number One.
>
> 'Get yourself a cola, my man,' said Number Two.

Mary's machine takes messages after she stops answering while Number One becomes increasingly machine-like in repeating his plea: 'I know you're there. Will you please pick up the phone?' occurs three times on consecutive lines (with a small variation), again like weird prose rhymes. Do they signify three separate telephone calls, perhaps suggesting greater intensity of feeling than Number One has let on? When Mary finally does answer, the lie that she tells about sleeping with someone else (in fact, she has a fantasy lover called Number Three) provokes Number Two into breaking off with 'Oh, God', and then 'the phone crashed, then hummed, the last verse of something long.' By the end, not communicating has not only become a strategy for Mary, but the work of the story has moved from recording voices that Mary's flatness of mood has turned into machine-like utterances to recording the absence of conversation: 'At home the phone rang, but Mary let the machine pick it up. It was nobody. The machine clicked and went through its business, rewound.' When the phone rings again two lines down, it is in a dream, with a little-known voice on the line saying 'I have some bad news.'

As conversations become emptied of emotion and meaning, Mary's own inner train of thought is increasingly conveyed in free indirect speech, and the gap between her inner and social voices, between her own life and the content of an unnamed book, grows more jarring.

> 'Oh,' said Mary, and opened her book again. The sun was beating down on the survivor. Blisters and sores. Poultices of algae paste. The water tight as glass and the wind blue-faced holding its breath. How did one get here? How did one's eye patched, rot-toothed life lead one along so cruelly, like a trick to the middle of the sea?

The nervous collapse into surreal image, foreshadowed at the beginning, has indeed been subtle, increasing disquiet conveyed entirely through adjustments to how voices are heard or not necessarily heard.

In Moore's story there are three actors but never truly more than one voice at a time. In George Saunders's 'Victory Lap', three actors and three voices create a coruscating, suspenseful account in real time of a near abduction and rape. All the action is vocalized, even more than focalized, through their stream of consciousness and the story is a marvel of technical accomplishment in plotting with a present-tense vividness. Everything that happens, and is then reported to have happened, occurs within the heads of the characters and no other narrator intrudes. Alone at home, Alison, the dreamy and spirited heroine, combines an adolescent, arch knowingness and dreamy naivety. The story takes it from the top with her physically at the top of the staircase of the family home. Mugging a diva-like grand entrance, she descends step-by-step while rehearsing balletic moves, her every move punctuated by phrases she recites from French classical dance vocabulary. Her thoughts circle round her world, and the sound of the doorbell scarcely punctures her reverie as she floats from the stairs to open the door to an assailant disguised as a worker bearing a knife. Before he can drag her across the front lawn to his van, she spies her geeky classmate and neighbour Kyle on the way home.

With a section change, we cut to Kyle as he enters Alison's peripheral vision and races home. His mind is a battleground of superego and id in which parental admonitions prescribing this precocious and perhaps even autistic only child's every gesture vie with an id overflowing with Tourette-like obscenities. Tethered to precise routine, he notices the odd goings-on across the street, registering the menacing look of the abductor and the weapon. The habit of obedience struggles with an urge to put things right, a rage at the disruption of order combined with affection for Alison, who is being shoved into a van. Just as he sets off with his toy weapon in hand, the perspective switches to that of the assailant, whose inner voice divulges how he stalked Alison (as well as a record of earlier crimes) up to and past the moment when Kyle bashes him on the head.

The technical accomplishment of the story lies not only—and perhaps even least—in the convergence of viewpoints on a single event. Like Ryunosuke Akutagawa in his reconstruction of a murder 'In a Bamboo Grove', Saunders provides multiple perspectives. But the resemblance ends there because epistemological uncertainty about truth, while dear to the Japanese master, is not an aim of Saunders's story. It is memorable, above all, because the lifelike rendering of American suburban speech idioms and a special state of adolescent consciousness, itself filled with the many voices of TV, parents, schoolteachers, and extra-curricular routines, constitute a diverse and wackily funny world.

The modern short story lends its ear to reported and quoted speech represented as conversations and interior monologues overheard, repeated, and interrupted. The performance element originally used in 19th-century tales as a frame to create atmosphere and setting, while much less common, remains available, and that is no surprise because the story gives a wonderful platform for invented personalities, whether socially conceived and typical of their time and place as in Yates, Saunders, and Moore, or tinged with something like a metaphysical principle of longing or justice as in Rhys, Jones, Joyce, and Malamud. None of their drama, humour, and wounded vitality would be palpable if they could not speak for themselves.

Chapter 4
Place

By comparison with novels, short stories generally underuse place. Few short story writers have achieved quite the indelible association with location celebrated in the work of novelists. To be sure, Warsaw, Harlem, and Jackson Mississippi provide setting and local character for I. B. Singer, Zora Neale Huston, and Eudora Welty, respectively, but the novels of Joyce, Bellow, Mann, and Auster completely inhabit Dublin, Chicago, Lübeck, and New York. Great short stories also gravitate toward personal predicament rather than the state of the nation: national questions that are vital to novels by Dostoevsky and Mann, for example, are not explored in their shorter works. Cycles of stories like Turgenev's *Sketches from a Hunter's Album* and Babel's *Red Cavalry*, Malamud's Fidelman stories, Welty's *The Golden Apples*, Gertrude Stein's *Three Lives*, and Steinbeck's *The Pastures of Heaven* are certainly not divorced from national histories. But customs, manners of speech, and situation root them in the local, bringing to life, respectively, Orel Province, Crimea, Mississippi, the invented Bridgeport, and Northern California. In the short story, environment tends to be passively present, easily reached to for context and shorthand association. Outside sci-fi (and Isaac Asimov's *Nightfall* would be a celebrated example), short stories are not in the business of creating places; nonetheless, there are certain places—cities, above all—that create stories. St Petersburg, a city whose history and liminal location spawned much urban folklore, has inspired an entire literary tradition.

Paris is another such place, and this chapter brings together a set of works that can be compared in how they use that city to condition the stories of their characters and plots. Paris represents an imaginative state that defines the fates of people who believe that living the Parisian dream can be a new reality. Enchantment and disenchantment with Paris shape stories in which the city exercises a spell, and Paris is more like a theatre set onto which drifters, dreamers, and charmers come in all ages and social classes. From long boulevards to public spaces like parks and cafés characters can be found scanning their future prospects somewhere in the distance. Paris is also a place of people-watching and sometimes rapid, sometimes troubled coupling, and the theme of romantic enchantment and disenchantment is often a common one linking the stories about Paris.

Bohemian Paradise

Paris, in literature, shifted from being the capital of Enlightenment to being the capital of mystery and criminality and remained fixed in this Romantic and melodramatic mode even after the physical city underwent modernization in the late 19th century. It is a hub for Balzac's stories of alchemists and conjurers (*The Skin of an Ass*) as well as dreamers and villains (across the epic cycle of his *Lost Illusions*), and the locus of the invention of the first great detective, even before Sherlock Holmes, namely, Dupin, the hero of Edgar Allan Poe's 1849 trilogy, 'The Murders in the Rue Morgue', 'The Mystery of Marie Roget', and 'The Purloined Letter'. Paris's literary identity thrived on dramatic social contrasts between an underworld and urbanity, and it featured madness, poverty, and dangerous schemers above ground and in the sewers. Charles Baudelaire's collection of fifty prose poems, *The Spleen of Paris* (1869, published posthumously), each of which has the quality of a report told in stream of consciousness, was perhaps the most vivid and sometimes grotesque evocation of the old Paris before its vast rebuilding by Haussmann, with kaleidoscopic and plotless snapshots of colourful bohemian types and decadent habits, a metropolis of intoxicated poverty-stricken dreamers. More bourgeois than proletariat, and more seekers of pleasure and artistic licence than Balzac's social climbers, Eugène Sue's plotters, or Poe's criminal artists, these melancholic romantic storytellers both gain and lose illusions in Paris.

Maupassant's short story 'A Parisian Adventure' concerns the wife of a country lawyer who, 'living where she did, viewed Paris as the apotheosis of glorious luxury and vice'. The boulevards that remain in modern fiction a typical feature of the city are here seen as an 'abyss of human passion'. The sex appeal of the modern city oozes not only from its material splendour but from its cultural status as a literary capital, and while attentive to objects marketed to the lower-middle classes, the heroine's hunt is for a lover who can write the sorts of fictions she consumes as a reader. A disingenuous *ingénue*, she outbids the writer standing next to her in a shop for a statue; her real aim is to gain his attention. She promises to surrender the statue to him if he will accompany her to her hotel in a carriage, and one thing leads to another. The morning after, the writer (who is certainly no Adonis) asks her to explain why she picked him up. The romance of desire conceived by a woman seduced by writing as the medium of 'excited dreams' cannot survive the glare of reality. The adventure, once concluded, looks like a fictional response to an opening line that sets out a thesis. It reeks of the way magazines flattered female readers of the day: 'Do women feel anything more keenly than curiosity?'

A different version of an answer to the same question can be found in Katherine Mansfield's 'Je ne parle pas français'. This is story as performance, street-theatre that comes pouring out of its voluble monologist seated in a seedy Paris café, on the prowl for 'the same strange types', those eccentrics remembered from Balzac and Baudelaire, the classic *flâneurs* (a fabled observer type who walks everywhere), who live in their dreams and frequent the café like old inhabitants. This extrovert character revels in sensationalizing his own emotional state with frank revelations. The unfeigned zaniness of his speech keeps the reader off-kilter. The story seems artless because all the experiential layers of biography are jumbled, and because the storyteller continually interrupts himself to comment on what he has just been saying, usually remarking the oddity of bringing 'the submerged' into the light. Volubility will characterize most Parisian stories: something in the setting brings out a love of exhibitionism. Mansfield's speaker could out-talk even Dostoevsky's famously garrulous underground man of whom he is a literary descendant: disaffected, overly emotional, consumed with regret even while denying it as 'an appalling waste of energy'. His Paris is a 'great trap set to catch innocents', and this monologue-cum-story is proof of the sophistication beyond years of someone who sets a trap.

The 26-year-old Raoul Duquette, an aspiring writer, calls himself 'a Parisian, a true Parisian'. He is to be taken at his own estimation as truly representative by being self-invented ('I date myself from the moment…'), by circumstance (living in a 'small bachelor flat' in a house that is not 'too shabby'), by creative activity as someone who writes for two newspapers, by vocation (being committed to serious literature), and by his conviction, like so many Parisian upstarts from the time of Balzac's heroes, that his own thoughts (or what he labels 'the mystery of the human soul') are the work of an individual genius. Archness and humour, while undoubtedly pleasing to the reader, also stimulate him to enjoy the spectacle he creates around his own identity. One has to wonder whether the performance or the truth matters more to the author of a book called *False Coins*. And, after all, toward the end of the story he wonders 'how one can look the part and not be the part? Or be the part and not look it? Isn't looking—being? Or being—looking?'

He stops short of completing the observation that 'all Parisians are more than half…' after revealing that he was initiated into erotic life at the age of 10 by a laundress, an African woman whose kisses repeated weekly remain a primal moment, anticipating a frank awareness of female desire spanning prostitutes, mistresses, and literary ladies of high respectability: 'I used to look across the table and think "Is that very distinguished young lady, discussing *le Kipling*, with the gentleman with the brown beard, really pressing my foot?"'

Being oversexed seems to be the condition of more than half of Paris, and his own sexual identity seems fluid in relation to an English couple, given the attraction he clearly feels for his male friend Dick Harmon ('All the while we were together Dick never went with a woman'). Despite hating the drink, Raoul orders a glass of whisky in order to write about the Englishman. A taciturn newspaper-man given to crooning songs about being hungry, Dick leaves Paris and then returns with a woman. Raoul sees through her pretence of being his mother, and concludes that they are lovers who wish him to join in to make a ménage à trois. 'Je ne parle pas français,' says she, while he thinks of the whole situation, their play-acting (with childlike names) and mixture of diffidence and decadence: 'It was too difficult, too English for me.' What the Parisian wants are not especially private passions but extrovert circus-like displays of exuberance, 'to hang out of the window and look for the hotel through the wrong end of a broken telescope, which was also a peculiarly ear-splitting trumpet'. Left high, if not dry, at the end by the couple, the speaker is about to depart when a woman takes a seat at his table and asks whether he has dined, even as a 'dirty old gallant' seated nearby wishes to pimp him 'a little girl'. In Paris there is always more.

Parisian dreamers

In literary Paris, making do with less never seems an affliction to anyone with some imagination. Mavis Gallant moved from

Canada to Paris in the 1950s and remained, over the years becoming one of the *New Yorker*'s most prolific contributors. Themes of personal and social dislocation run through her many collections. Early stories feature emotionally neglected children. Her Paris stories are inhabited by solitary individuals, marginal people whether by dint of race, status, wealth, or age. Often foreigners, they are awkward people who fit awkwardly with their host country. Impoverished, they often face material and psychological challenges that drive them to dreams of escape. Gallant gravitates to characters situated between the bohemian and the bourgeois, the fantasy life of the *flâneur* and worldly awareness, the marital and extra-marital. No population could better bear out Frank O'Connor's famous (if overstated) claim that the short story genre was made for the submerged classes.

Mansfield's Raoul sees no real division between his life and art. Sandor Speck, the hero of Gallant's 'Speck's Idea', is a second-generation Parisian art dealer who embellishes the biography of one of his painters in order to sex up the provenance of minor paintings. His business ought to be filling his clients' lives (and walls) with art; in fact, his gift is for con artistry. Although Gallant doesn't date the story, references to Basque separatist terror bombings, insurgent Communist students, and the demolition of city-centre slums point to the late 1960s and early 1970s. Events force Speck to move his gallery three times, finally to a smart location in the 7th arrondissement next to ministries and a Fascist bookseller, whose window is smashed by radicals from time to time. Speck by name and a speck in the history of art, he remains sublimely aloof to political unrest (his modest stock of paintings escapes the vandals). If anything, the cultural malaise filling the newspapers that Speck reads stimulates his imagination. Parisian highbrows, as the story observes, are given to seeing everywhere, and especially in cultural decline, a mystery, the solution to which must be some elaborate conspiracy invisibly plotted. Low on clients and on stock (his current exhibition is on the influence of the Parisian school on Romanian painting in 1931–2), Speck imagines the sort of exhibition that would shake up the art market, a sensational discovery that would offset a malaise hanging over Paris with the discovery of a hidden talent. Like all the rest of the Parisian dreamers, something in the city makes him want to be the star in his own adventure.

Descriptions of rainy streets contribute to the colour palette of many a Parisian story, supplemented by glimpses of this consumer, luxury city. Here, more unusually, 'the street resembled a set in a French film, designed for export, what with the policemen's white rain capes aesthetically gleaming and the lights of the bookstore, the restaurant, and the gallery reflected, quivering European-looking puddles'. The idea that puddles can have a provenance could only exist in the mind of an art-dealer determined to monetize even the most prosaic images (Speck's line is in barges, bridges, cafés, twilights, those favoured liminal spaces of spectators on the city and its street life). Capes on police require a caper. While a few 'determined intellectuals slink, wet, into the Métro', Speck, who cannot afford the central heating in his gallery, drives a Rolls-Royce; and while he is an atheist, he believes that 'the Grand Architect, if he was any sort of omnipresence worth considering, knew exactly what Speck needed now'. He likes his clients to provide 'crisp, dry banknotes' but adores the sweet, sticky, moist soft macaroons, stuffed brioches, and more to be bought 'in the finest pastry shops in Paris'. Even here we might feel that Speck, like other Parisian mavericks, never quite adds up, since the name of this Central European scion is German for 'bacon'. He turns logic upside down by musing about the ideal life and work of an artist needed for his times, and if the artist doesn't exist, he will have to be invented to enlarge Speck.

That requires a plot. Into the life of every Parisian dreamer an accident of chance must fall. At a grand soirée, Speck overhears an elderly senator mention to someone that it is time to get rid of his 'Cruches'. The light goes on in Speck's brain—or, as Gallant puts it mock portentously, the Grand Architect of the Universe just rapped him over the head—and he cries out, 'Don't sell! Hang on! Cruche is coming back!' Cometh the hour, cometh the con artist as Speck determines to create an artist and body of work out of Cruche to suit the mood music that will open the market. *Cruche* is the French word for a 'pot' or 'empty vessel'. If the Grand Architect needed a partner it would be this Small Artist and a Speck to fill that empty vessel. Speck meets his match in Lydia, Cruche's widow, a Scottish member of an obscure Christian sect (her surname is virtually an anagram for church, after all) claiming to be the true Israelites and living in border country. While Speck swindles the establishment, Lydia plays her part by finding a Milanese dealer to create a bidding war. 'Cruche is mine. He was my idea. No one can have my idea,' claims Speck. In a story about the invention of an artist who in fact existed, it is not surprising that life should seem stranger than art, and Speck is ultimately proved right in a world in which the rules of the fantasist apply with a surreal logic—or right at least in his own mind when he leaves Paris. Catalogue in hand with his forged autograph, he crosses the Alps like some ham Napoleon.

Dreamers come in all sizes. Another class of Parisian dreamers will be the urchins or the *gamins*. Young ragamuffins, innocents abroad in their own city, they are celebrated in French Romantic fiction by Victor Hugo in *Les Misérables*, later in popular culture by *chansonniers* like Yves Montand ('Un gamin d'Paris, c'est tout un poème'), film-makers (François Truffaut's *Four Hundred Blows* 1960) and in literature by André Gide and Valéry Larbaud. These are not artful dodgers or exploited youths as in *Oliver Twist* but, in the words of the song, adolescent 'mixtures of angel and devil' who evade authority and hate school because street life appeals to their innate spiritedness, the French *esprit* that stands for quick-wittedness and vivacity.

This is the outlook of the autobiographical hero of Georges Perec's 'The Runaway', a rare short story from an OULIPO writer renowned for applying contrived linguistic rules to writing. The chronological opening of the story is displaced from the start. Like frames out of order in a film, time and space are slightly dislocated since the narrator will explain only after two pages that the hero is skipping school, and, several pages after that, detail the boy's itinerary, and only after that reveal his home address and the exact date (11 May 1947). This onion-like growth of the story away from the single point of consciousness to social reality mimics the boy's own vision of Paris as concentric and his circular movements. 'Heady with freedom' before nine o'clock, this cerebral *gamin* devises ways to avoid going to school, and works out that the likely penalty of two hours in detention will be shorter than his liberation in Paris. He contemplates raising some cash by selling some of the more precious stamps from his collection, probably just an idle fancy since he loiters near the stamp market on a Wednesday, knowing that it is closed. He clearly dreams of wider adventures, captured in his gesture of tracing circles in yellow on the wooden bench on which he sits near the puppet theatre and eventually falls asleep in the cold.

Somewhere between the start of the school-day and being found by a stranger and taken to the police, he has bought and read a comic book, drunk water from a fountain, and his reveries, as befits a Perec alter ego, are word-obsessed. While the mirrors of the flat where he lives with his aunt and uncle disquiet him with reflections of himself into infinity, he finds tranquillity in a street named for a different type of religious infinity, the Rue de l'Assomption. It is not religious consolation, however, that he seeks in the thought of the everlasting life of the Virgin, or even a nearby church in which to sit, but rather the fact that the dustbins have not been emptied. The Paris he sees is full of signs. There is the 'F' in the sign on the headquarters of the newspaper *Le Figaro*, and there are the newspapers he pulls out of the rubbish bins, which he reads for the sport pages and gossip. He clearly enjoys them more than any schoolwork, but above all he loves joining another class of people, the 'readers who linger for hours reading the *Figaro*, the *Figaro littéraire*, and the *Figaro agricole*'. This is a Paris whose brainwork is inseparable from the dream-work of fantasists. Benches are the prominent landmarks, noted in métro stations, in parks, among shrubs, and on streets, because they afford all the space required by Parisian dreamers once they emerge from their garret.

Enchantment dispelled

Fortune hunters of a different kind have a Parisian pedigree. Long before Hemingway made Paris an expat capital between the wars, Henry James and Edith Wharton had identified the city as a welcome home for down-at-heel Americans whose breeding outstripped their means. The ambience of the city is easily assimilated by Parisian transplants of the right mindset, often the exiles and natural vagrants to be found in the stories of Mansfield and Gallant. But the city can also shock the innocence of visitors, and the tension between being seduced and resisting the city's illusions is borne out in many a marriage plot set in Paris.

Edith Wharton's 'The Last Asset' centres on a scheme hatched by the extravagant but broke Mrs Sam Newell to marry off her daughter to a French aristocrat. Once everything has been arranged, the nobleman insists that the girl's father, an American businessman who lost his fortune and has been long estranged from his wife and daughter, be produced. Mrs Newell calls on the main character, a newspaper-man friend called Garnett, to find her former husband and rope him into appearing at the wedding. His presence at the wedding of their daughter is valuable because it provides social respectability, the only gift he can afford. Garnett tracks down old man Newell to a 'dingy hotel in the Latin quarter' that reminds one of the bohemian garret popular in the 1850s that remains a particular Parisian feature. Its attraction is its anonymity and its proximity to a 'cheap and excellent restaurant'. Like Perec's runaway, old man Newell enjoys a park bench, his perch for feeding the sparrows, but he also values the fact that the city proves a perfect place for someone of his detachment, a natural place for the marginal person on whom 'it makes little impression' and tolerant of 'that odd American astuteness which seems the fruit of innocence rather than of experience'. In this case, the innocent abroad is not at the mercy of corrupt foreigners, but of an American wife who can out-swindle the most louche aristocrats.

In 'Madame de Mauves', Henry James creates a variation on the theme of the American innocent he made famous in *Daisy Miller* and explored on a novelistic scale in *Portrait of a Lady* and *The Ambassadors*. The story, as many set specifically in Paris do, develops a love triangle between Longmore, a young American of leisure, the wealthy American heroine, Euphemia, who is convent educated, a dreamy girl besotted with the heroes of chivalric fictions and whose innocence is her striking feature, and her promiscuous husband, the count. Like a fairy-tale princess, she has a turret chamber in her house where she writes to her mother. They live unhappily since the count 'was a pagan and his wife a Christian'. His blatant infidelity only encourages Longmore's worshipping of Euphemia. In its handling of the themes of sexual jealousy and virtue as a weapon, the story owes something to French libertine fiction, especially Laclos's *Dangerous Liaisons*. The count would be all too happy to see his wife compromised by a dalliance, and he encourages Longmore, also acting through his patently unpleasant sister, a Madame Clairin (possibly named for the famous actress Mlle Clairon as she enters and exits with great dramatic flair), who defends the right of the aristocrat to have liaisons 'as great traditions and charming precedents', belittles her sister-in-law as a 'little American bourgeoise', and manipulates Longmore. In the end, the countess has the upper hand and exacts her justice.

Paris throughout is admired as a pleasure ground, elegant and popular, and the story repeatedly juxtaposes its 'turfy avenues' and glades and the 'boulevards'. The city is kept at a distance since the countess's estate is in the nearby suburb of Saint-Germain, and Longmore makes the long journey on foot as though shaking off the taint of Paris morality before entering the zone of 'the lonely lady of Saint-German' as he regards her. Those glades serve as spaces of retreat and restoration of innocence. James has symbolically divided urban geography into Euphemia's zone, an 'artificial garden' with alleys and a fountain, much like a painting by Fragonard in which gentle flirtation and civilized conversation take place. She tells Longmore that 'France is out there beyond the garden' whereas her garden is her own little country.

At one point, Euphemia suggests to Longmore when they are walking that 'our arbour here' should be their 'sensible country'. For Longmore, not to be in Paris would be to 'miss some thrilling chapter of experience', meaning that he is culturally programmed to seek out some romance, and in confessing his admiration he identifies the 'distant city' as a 'potent force' that conditions his attitude, a place that is also 'necessary' to her husband. There is another countryside described in the story, a wonderful vista like a painting by Corot of 'cool, metallic green' and an atmosphere of light, a space that Longmore enters and regards as the most characteristically French landscape he has seen, one read about in novels and admired on canvases. Here, when he stops at an inn he meets a French painter and a young woman referred to as his wife. But the innkeeper reveals that the girl is not his wife. The appearance of the painter is only a cameo but it is significant because he is portrayed as 'evidently a member of that jovial fraternity of artists whose very shabbiness has an affinity with the unestablished and unexpected in life', as the narrator says.

The varnish of the American romance with Paris comes off in the shabby atmosphere of Richard Ford's 'Occidentals'. The story brings together the prominent themes associated with Paris: the expat experience of Americans, love and death, creative renewal, and self-invention. The city's geography and landmarks are explicitly evoked, even listed, because of their 'power over the imaginations' of the two main characters. To American literary types, there are no more famous places than the constellation of cafés and streets on the Left Bank. The paradoxical feeling of being foreign to one's own culture and tempted to imagine oneself into another preoccupies Charley Matthews, the story's hero. His companion on the trip is Helen Carmichael, a sparky ex-showgirl and former student with whom he's struck up a sexual liaison. Author of a single novel, former college professor, Charley has turned his back on the family business in order to pursue his writing and is fastidiously diffident in everything, including his status as an author. At once relentlessly realistic and in love with the myth of the city, he fails to see what is right in front of him and experiences Paris as a tension between the beautiful and the ugly. Nothing, whether a landscape, relationship, or meal, can be just one or the other, which seems appropriate for Charley who is, after all, the author of *The Predicament*.

All would be well for him as a tourist if the Parisian myth stopped breaking down at every stage. Charley is there to meet the French publisher of a translation of his novel, something that strikes him as improbable since it 'depicted ordinary, idle-class people caught in the grip of small, internal dilemmas of their own messy concoction'. When he and Helen arrive in Paris just before Christmas, it is only to discover that the publisher has blithely decamped with his family on a tropical holiday and his translator is also nowhere to be found. Paris contains the vistas of which he dreams, including boat rides on the Seine and long walks through the Bois de Boulogne, but the hotel where he and Helen stay is run-down and, more portentously, overlooks the Montparnasse Cemetery. As Charley observes, this Paris seems 'baffling' and 'might as well have been East Berlin'. He has a kinship with old Mr Newell in Wharton's story, at ease with the fantasy of eking out a modest life as a non-French-speaking observer, another down-at-heel American. Like the heroine of Maupassant's 'A Parisian Adventure', he entertains a fantasy of rekindling an affair with a woman from his past, but just loses his nerve about a tryst when he calls her. Even like the boy protagonist of Perec's story, he finds freedom in roaming the streets of Paris, but he also tires of the rain and 'glassy puddles' and finds it impossible to get his bearings on the map: the Eiffel Tower is 'the miracle of the Occident' and Helen and Charley when enthralled by Paris and at their best are self-proclaimed Occidentals. But the Eiffel Tower proves useless as a landmark when Charley walks around the city. Beauty and utility seem to occupy separate spheres, and the artist in Charley should perhaps know better than to try to reconcile the aesthetic and practical.

The Paris that lives up to the dream and the Paris that disappoints are both there. It is not surprising that the seediness and dirt that are such features of literary Paris offend other tourists expecting the ideal. The main pair, however, are different. Charley, like the French characters, is marked out as 'eccentric' and has the artist's outsider view. He might qualify as the type of American who could make it in France, like the generation of Hemingway whom the 'French made feel at home in a way their own countrymen hadn't'. The French strike Charley as amateur actors playing French people. His poor French proves to be an advantage as it gives licence to invent his own script. Helen is more at ease because she wishes to hold fast to life. 'The French are more serious than we are. They care more. They have a perspective on importance and unimportance. You can't become them. You just have to be happy being yourself.' Each sees a very different Paris. She has a capacity to block out the ugly as unnecessary, to make it invisible, just as Ford delays the revelation to the reader and Charley of the knowledge that she is in fact dying.

There is perhaps a cost to Charley's state of bemusement, since it blinds him from seeing that the French are not playing at being French, and that Helen's strained behaviour is the effect of her illness. He misreads her talking about where she will be buried as fantasy, whereas in fact the question is more urgent than he realizes. In their hotel they both live in the shadow of death figured on the wall of the Montparnasse Cemetery. On their first night, the jet-lagged Charley observes a beggar go over the wall to find shelter, musing that most people would rather stay out of cemeteries. Improbable though it is, Helen is the heroic one, the daughter of an obsessive admirer of Napoleon and also a reader of Baudelaire who would like to be buried near the poet (as her body becomes increasingly covered in bruises she seems to bear on her skin *les fleurs du mal*).

The trip to Paris, with its fateful ending, marks a stage in a sentimental education. Charley does finally meet his translator, Madame de Grenelle, who appreciated his book because it 'has the ring of actuality'. And the linguistic and cultural actuality that she explains is that the French language has no word for 'predicament'. Her view is that his book will be better in French than in English, because it will be humorous—that is, it will incorporate the French perspective on unimportance that Helen observed. Placed at the end of the story, this conversation marks a new relationship while replaying the earlier exchange between Helen and Charley on how the French and Americans see one another. Being French turns out not to be a matter of nationality, but a state of understanding: to be serious one has also to be amusing. This understanding, which Charley must discover for himself, is one that Mansfield's hero took as a given. Charley muses that his purpose on the trip is 'not to convert anything to a commodity he could take back but to suit himself to the unexpected, to what was already here'. If the story does not strive toward epiphanies, a portrait of the artist as a middle-aged man coalesces. Paris rubs off on Charley, who joins the ranks of the heroes of other Parisian tales because his translation into French is both linguistic and attitudinal, something Helen failed to achieve in her adamance on being an outsider.

Each of these stories, from Maupassant to Ford, and including Gallant, Mansfield, and James, reveals characters striving to find in Paris an escape from a present condition into a more fluid state.

Regardless of the obstacles they encounter, and whether they have the mature cynicism of Maupassant's heroine or the naive directness of Perec's youth, the city encourages an illusion of the unlimitedness of life. This is because, for both native and outsider, Paris is a place where one takes one's life as art and one's art as life. The multiplicity of forms the city takes in its statuary, parks, artwork, and highly codified human interactions, gives the impression to characters that their lives have the substantiality of art even as their stories expose the fragility of that illusion.

Chapter 5
The plot thickens . . . and thins

For much of the 19th century, anecdote and incident inspired short fiction written for a mass market. The incident or anecdote-based short story made a virtue of brevity, and the economy of style and consequential arrangement of causes and effects well suited slice-of-life episodes, criminal capers, the sensational, and the supernatural. All these modes are staples of its history. What they all share is a skill in building up suspense that must be relieved and establishing dread that must be left to linger. Yet we shall also see that the genre has been enjoying a long postmodernist reincarnation in which it has adopted almost the opposite approach. Losing the plot has been a source of fictional experimentation and liberation from linearity. What is left is writing in which the making of the story is its own subject. Like serialism in music, repetition with subtle variation has become a key structure, with added effects of reversal, rewriting, and multiplied outcomes. Storytelling as a type of play can revel in relativizing the truth of fiction and the notion of fiction as truth, all of which has consequences for the plot.

'Keep 'em guessing'

The success of genre fiction depends mostly on good plotting. Literary fiction, while technically and thematically more complex and stylish, has acquired from genre fiction devices and effects in fabricating suspense. As John Updike said in an interview of 2004, 'All those mystery novels I read taught me something about keeping the plot taut.' And genre fiction has staked valid claims to quality beyond a mass market. While a master of detective speak and a noir idiom, Dashiell Hammett toned down slangy writing to focus on the PI's investigative practices pursued against a background world of mayhem and political corruption imbued with serious social critique. Hammett's Continental Op stories, originally published from 1923 onwards in the magazine *Black Mask*, were conceived as puzzle plot stories, sometimes of great ingenuity, and would fail to satisfy readers if their criminal schemes took a back seat. In this respect they live up to the criteria for ingenious detection set by Edgar Allan Poe in his pioneering detective fictions like 'The Murders in the Rue Morgue' and tales of suspense like 'Cask of Amontillado'. Similarly, in their attention to psychology and point of view, great writers of ghost stories, such as Edith Wharton, E. F. Benson, M. R. James, and Henry James, of detective stories, such as Conan Doyle and Dashiell Hammett, or of confessional stories like Bernard Malamud, also excel at the technicalities of plot, while adding a whole extra dimension of psychology.

A tradition of spin-offs and cross-overs continues to be found in unexpected places. In Edward P. Jones's 'All Aunt Hagar's Children', the protagonist is a soldier newly returned from the Korean War holding a temporary summer job doing minor investigative work for a Jewish lawyer. A version of a classic gumshoe like Chandler's Lew Archer, the narrator is inveigled by his formidable mother and two aunts into solving the murder of a cousin. They have their own back-story, a subplot of retribution giving depth to their current pursuit of justice. But peripheral yarns, told with folkloric touches, elevate the violence of everyday life into saga. The narrator hears the mysterious last words of a lady who dies in his arms when they are riding a trolley. Haunted by the words, phonetically transcribed, he mutters them aloud one day and they catch the ear of the boss's wife, who recognizes them as a pair of Yiddish phrases. If the delicious coincidence is a parodic send-up of sleuthing, finding the key to one mystery seems to unlock his wits as the story comes back to the original problem of who killed cousin Ike, which brings its own twist.

The influence of Anglo-American potboilers and ghost stories was international and extensive. The Japanese master Ryunosuke Akutagawa remains most famous for 'In a Bamboo Grove' (1921; later the basis of the classic film *Rashomon* by Akira Kurosawa), a crime mystery, confession, and ghost story in one. A warrior-husband and his wife enter a grove, possibly lured there by a bandit, Tajomaru. The husband's murder is the story's one incontestable fact. The identity of the culprit remains uncertain and finally unknowable because three characters claim to be the killer. The story consists of testimonies and confessions. The former are offered by a woodcutter, a priest, a policeman near the scene, as well as the wife's mother (as a character witness). None of these witnesses is directly involved: they add circumstantial details to the confessions of the bandit, widow and victim, all suspected of the murder.

Whodunits such as this story ought, by definition, to drive toward a solution. Its opening words in English are 'That is true', as spoken by the woodcutter who found the body. Readers expecting the weight of the evidence and the credibility of the witnesses to confute lies will be disappointed since the rival accounts seem equally plausible and none actively contests the other. The bandit claims that he had no intention of murdering the husband after raping the wife. The wife abhors the thought that there were two witnesses to her deep shame and insists that the two men had a sword fight in which the bandit won, making the bandit a killer if not a murderer. However, in her statement the wife contradicts this by acknowledging her rape and omitting to mention the duel. Instead, she claims that her husband's hatred aggravated her dishonour, and that he regarded her with a 'cold look of contempt and hatred'. In her statement, she claims to have avenged herself by killing him. Having exonerated the bandit, she professes her own guilt. But matters do not rest there, because the husband's spirit comes forward with his own account. He recounts how the bandit expressed his infatuation with the wife, who suddenly turned on her husband, uttered 'hateful words' about him, and ordered the bandit to 'kill him'. Instead of obeying, the bandit cast the wife off and asked the husband what he should do. At that moment the wife ran off and the bandit disappeared. Despairing of her hatred, the husband claims that he took his own life.

'In a Bamboo Grove' eliminates the role of the detective, leaving it to the reader to ponder equally plausible accounts about lust, honour, and shame as motivations (the mother's letter corroborates the wife's description of her own feelings about besmirched honour). In the bandit's and husband's confessions the wife has instigated the crime. In the wife's account, she is a victim of abuse and her actions justified. Her true nature, rather than the culpability of the bandit, is the mystery that shifts this from being a procedural investigation to an extra-judicial character judgement. While the identity of the actual killer remains unknowable, her role, informed by her outraged shame, is pivotal in each of the several plots that readers can review when considering what really happened without ever truly knowing.

A 'keep 'em guessing' uncertainty about the culprit postpones come-uppance, though sometimes not for very long. In Maupassant or Muriel Spark, the shocking turning point achieves a form of justice—cruel, commensurate, and, ironically, often the opposite of the perpetrators' goal (riches to rags in the former's 'The Necklace'), and writers in this vein share with pulp fiction a zeal for entertainment and catharsis.

Another variation on the suspenseful plot is not about who and when, but *why*. More ambitious, and therefore usually longer, these stories often use a trivial incident, such as an accidental find or encounter, from which wider consequences unravel, tapping into local gossip or chain reactions to explore that element of 'why'. It takes no more than a chance event, such as the finding of a financial document in Tolstoy's *The Purloined Coupon*, to unleash a whole sequence of devastating mistakes; and no more than a chance conversation in Eudora Welty's 'Why I Live at the P.O.' to spin a story about a much larger occurrence. In the opening of Alice Munro's 'The Love of a Good Woman', a group of school friends, out for an innocent day on the river, discover the local optician drowned in his car underwater. How and why this came about will only be explained—if it has been truly explained—much later as the narrative loops back in time to the day of the accident and then moves forward into the present. Almost the entire first part is given over to describing the boys' families and home lives. By design, Munro delays the story's revelations as long as possible, controlling the pace masterfully to intensify the drama of one plot and the sudden determination of one character to change her own life. In fact, the clue to the crime lies on the first page in a use of detail worthy of a detective fiction. The scrambling of the order of events obscures the true nature of a plot that is less about dying than about a killing, in which moral reckoning remains only implied in an ominous silence.

A dreadful aesthetic

Accidents of circumstance set plots in motion for Tolstoy, Welty, and Munro that are fully realized and come to an end after the event. Stories of dread specialize in finding how cleverly the ordinary can be used to mask the dreadful before the worst occurs. The English writer Elizabeth Taylor, usually appreciated for the shrewd comedy of her portrayal of eccentrics, had a flair for the ominous as well. 'Fly Paper' is an object lesson in the creation of dread, a very short story of Hitchcockian power. Its balance between portentous hints and minutely observed description confers both the shock of pulp and the quality of literary fiction. 'Who or what is the fly?' is the question posed from the start. Sylvia rides the bus to her music lesson on the way back from school. Orphaned young, and not a very gifted musician, she lives with her grandmother and chafes at her overbearing nannying. Hating the dark of winter interiors, she also dislikes being swaddled in her overwarm coat. Sylvia has been warned not to talk to strangers. But since her mother's death she has grown sullen, suggesting that she feels unloved. Unloved children are vulnerable.

Copious use of physical detail that would seem ordinary to realism creates a seedy atmosphere, a tone of slight unpleasantness. Sylvia is not, the narrator makes clear, a lovely child (her hair is greasy and she sweats), the bus is not especially comfortable (it seems to 'tremble and jingle'), and the only other passengers are an odd pair. Behind her sits a very tall man whose hair 'is carefully arranged over his bald skull'. He strikes up a conversation with Sylvia by observing that it is hot, meaning he has noticed that she has unbuttoned her coat. She blushes and turns away, repeatedly ignoring his further pestering, dressed up in oily politeness. ('"I hope you don't mind me chatting to you," the man said to Sylvia, "I am fond of children. I am known as being *good* with them."') She divulges her name and in a grotesque touch, he bursts out eccentrically into a refrain of the Shakespearian love song 'Who is Sylvia? What is she-he?' Put on her guard, Sylvia finds an ally in the third passenger, a woman who sits at the front, and exasperatedly berates the man to leave her alone. Certain verbal repetitions and lingering over details poison the atmosphere without looking like explicit clues to the switch and bait that is happening. Sylvia must be at an age when she outgrows her clothes quickly. She feels self-conscious that the hem on her skirt, already let down once, is now too short. The bus, meanwhile, has reached the 'outskirts of the town'. Why does it matter that 'its outskirts were quiet'?

It is rather noisy on the bus because of the male busybody and when they reach the next stop Sylvia realizes that she is early and has time to spare. She decides to get off and walk the rest of the way, slowing her pace to enter a shop. The man from the bus has also descended and offers to buy her an ice. She shrugs him off and at that point is also caught up by the woman from the bus who admonishes her not to talk to strangers. Feeling terribly constrained by life and having 'no faith in freeing herself from it', and now trusting a woman who seems to have her interests at heart, Sylvia accepts her invitation to stop for a cup of tea at her house nearby before she walks the rest of the way. Sylvia remembers her grandmother's warning, 'cautionary tales, dark with unpleasant hints', but the woman from the bus chases the man away, threatening to call a policeman if he does not take a different direction. 'You can't be too careful,' the woman says as they make their way along quite a desolate road. At this point will readers expect the tension built up around the pestering man to be defused? Can the story simply be about a Good Samaritan and an unhappy girl?

A nice cup of tea awaits Sylvia in a house at the edge of a wasteland. The 'frilly, looped up curtains, with plastic flowers' are reminiscent of the earlier seediness; and perhaps also of the dangerous lure of a gingerbread house from Hansel and Gretel. Sylvia spots a budgie in a cage and is drawn to the bird. She waits for tea, standing by the table, and also notices the fly-paper on which 'some of the flies were still half alive, and striving hopelessly to free themselves'. The story has only a few lines left to run, and Taylor, with brilliant economy, captures the horror dawning on Sylvia when she counts three places laid for tea, and hears Mabel open the front door for her husband, Herbert. We can all now see who Herbert is, and what Mabel means when she says, a little impatiently, 'It's all ready.' The title, the creepy stalking, the physical details, observed by a narrator with a perhaps unhealthily close eye, should have put the reader on edge. Dread emanates not solely from the certainty that something awful must either occur or be averted; it stems from the double awareness that however prepared one might be one cannot see it coming until it hits. No crime has been committed, at least not yet. Sylvia's entrapment is a story about the insidious ordinariness of an evil couple. What stories of horror, the supernatural, and the surreal have in common is their use of dread as an aesthetic effect, best sustained in a form like the story because its creation must be efficient and stealthy. Sylvia's horror at falling into a trap is akin to the gradual dread the Governess feels in Henry James's classic 'The Turn of the Screw'. What crime fiction, horror, and the supernatural share is an eagerness to glimpse the half-seen forces of evil lurking, preying on the psychic states of characters and readers.

Fables of the human condition

Dread can also contribute to stories about the human condition under duress more fundamentally. Actors in fictions of an existential slant will struggle against injustice caused by bad people, a corrupt system, or a godless world; yet the reasons for such malevolent action seem almost as unfathomable as supernatural effects. Few stories capture more brutally and forlornly the reality of political violence than Jean-Paul Sartre's 'The Wall' ('Le Mur', 1939) set during the Spanish Civil War. A prisoner, Pablo Ibbieta, awaits execution and considers the value of life and whether it is worth betraying his principles to give the Fascists the information they want in exchange for his release. The exhausted Pablo does not relent until at the last minute he gives his captors false information about the location of a comrade they are hunting down, unaware that his friend has changed hiding places and has now been betrayed. Through its plot twist, a story about political violence acquires another dimension as a fable of existentialism and the human condition as a trap.

In works about existential struggle, focused on consciousness in the moment of strategizing survival or in savouring rations, endings are often rhetorically flat. Since all outcomes tend to be about life and death, plots can be more engaging for the intricate stages of awareness and reaction that they entail than for their resolution, although it will be sometimes at the very end of a story that the reasons for survival, sometimes invisible to the actors, are told. What sort of plot can there be in a prison system where the exploitation of labour has become routine? The Gulag was a space in which illusions of control were fleeting attempts to exploit tiny chances of gain or survival. With no expectations of new outcomes, resignation rather than dread is the typical attitude.

'Shmeliov's brigade was a dumping ground for human slag, the waste people from the gold-mine pit face' is how Shalamov's 'The Lawyers' Conspiracy' begins. The whole story is about the bureaucratic task of sifting out lawyers from the prison population, presumably for execution. Andreyev is pulled out of the barracks to answer a summons by prosecutor Romanov. Trying to catch him out, he is asked about his profession (lawyer) and whether he knows two other people (Parfentiev and Vinogradov, also lawyers). He is then sent off on a series of journeys in trucks and cars at temperatures of minus 60 degrees. These take many hours without going very far, and they lead to days spent waiting in detention cells interrupted by low-key enquiries or confessions. When three men, also sentenced to death, join them, the group is moved to another special prison, transferred by yet another truck in the morning. 'Where are they taking us?' I asked. 'I don't know where they're taking you, but I'm going to Magadan. To be shot.' Several interrogations, uniformly administered, steep the story in the logic of prison bureaucracy.

Shalamov engineers a stunning plot reversal at the very end. Awaiting execution, Andreyev finds himself next to a certain Parfentiev. The two names brought up at the opening have finally fallen into place as both these prisoners join seven other men in the guard-house. Against expectation they are all released. They are then told that Captain Rebrov, the last officer to interrogate them, has been arrested. This reverses the ostensible logic of the plot. The conspirators of the title are not the men who have been rounded up and expect to die. The conspirators have brought trumped-up charges against that group in order to turn the tables on Rebrov, who was the secret target all along.

If Shalamov's world is a nightmare come true, Kafka's is a waking dream in which fear is expressed through odd gestures and startling images. Like 'The Lawyers' Conspiracy', 'A Country Doctor' describes a state of perplexity. It is a world in which the relation between cause and effect has become attenuated, causing permanent bafflement, captured aphoristically in relation to what inflicted a wound: 'Many a one proffers his side and can hardly hear the axe in the forest, far less that it is coming nearer to him.' The speaker becomes embroiled in someone else's story while the action of most importance to him happens somewhere else. A country doctor has been summoned to attend to a young boy during a blizzard. His horse dies and a mysterious groom musters a pair of horses to draw his carriage. The young boy aggressively kisses Rosa, the housemaid, to the chagrin of the doctor. Deflection onto incidentals like details of transport—the lorry in Shalamov, the two exalted horses in Kafka—matter more than the journey itself because in each of these stories scenes dissolve into one another to disorientating effect. As Kafka's patient says to the doctor (in Michael Hoffman's translation), 'You've just snowed in from somewhere yourself, it's not as though you got here under your own steam.'

He arrives at his destination, increasingly preoccupied with the likelihood that Rosa may be raped in his absence. Initially he dismisses the patient, unable to examine the boy properly because his thoughts turn to Rosa. He looks again, however, and discovers a wound that is rose-red: the 'flower in the side' pullulates with 'roseate worms': at the level of symbolic language, this is a second wounded rose and the transference of his anxiety about Rosa's deflowering onto the boy's body, the fear of sexual transgression extended into the fantasy that he has been stripped by the family and laid in the patient's bed. As in everyday reality, the family hover about the bed; however, in the absurdist nightmare they sing a menacing song.

There is a burden of blame directed at the doctor that he has already assumed as guilt, acting as though he has caused the malevolent materialization of groom, the boy's wound, and Rosa's misfortune, all because he answered 'the false alarm of the night bell'—false either because he cannot cure the boy or because it distracted him from the horror he could prevent. His confidence shattered, the doctor tries to placate the young boy and then to escape, seemingly without dressing, eager 'not to waste time'. In these stories by Shalamov and Kafka, space contracts to the immediate field of vision, the world even just beyond disappearing into the darkness of night. Kafka's final tableau is of the doctor, whose progress home seems to be at a standstill. 'Betrayed! Betrayed!' he cries, bemoaning the recognition that whatever has happened, the cause of the wound, the fear of rape, cannot be assuaged; and because his horses cannot gallop, he wanders. Is the failure really his?

Losing the plot

Fables of the human condition reveal the impossibility or at least the difficulty of finding the agents of truth in a universe governed by an opaque causality. An alternative to these fictions is stories that evade existential entrapment through sheer playfulness. From the second half of the 20th century, plot in world literature has often meant play, as can be seen in the play with identity central to the works of Julio Cortázar in Spain and Guillermo Cabrera Infante in Cuba, or writers like the Frenchman Raymond Queneau and Italian Italo Calvino, influenced by the experimentalism of OULIPO (*Ouvroir de littérature potentielle*), or American postmodernists such as Donald Barthelme and Donald Antrim. Resistant to hierarchies that are patriarchal or colonial or gendered, storytellers have moved away from finality—and even, sometimes, from getting started.

Play serves a higher truth than mere games, and often reflects on its own rules. Postmodernism as a movement was committed to relativizing truth by exposing the viewpoint (and prejudices) behind absolutist philosophical positions. Short stories can delight as head-games. Unlike stories that use plot to test characters, short stories of this stripe use character to test plot. Language and device can dominate; plots thin out rather than thicken because the sequence in which events occur counts for less than the manipulation of perceptions of truth and the experience of time. In carrying over that newfound uncertainty about certainty, postmodern fiction applied two seminal lessons taught by the Russian Formalists: that works of fiction could play off the events as they must have happened (*fabula*) and the order of those events in the narration (*siuzhet*); and that stories, when they included a metafictional element laying bare their very artificiality, did not forfeit their power of illusion because reader psychology could be quite supple and adjust within the premises set out by the fiction. Realism and anti-realism coiled round one another.

How many actions and actors does it take to make a story? How original does plot have to be, and can literary (as opposed to pulp) fiction succeed when recycling well-worn plots? In his miniature story 'The Plot', Jorge Luis Borges writes that 'Fate is partial to repetitions, variations, symmetries', a suggestion that even destiny limits outcomes according to a fixed number of permutations. And yet readers with an interest in murder, for instance, may take satisfaction in multiple treatments: Julius Caesar may be the hero of plays by both Shakespeare and Quevedo, and while neither can change his death, which is an ineluctable historical fact, they can construct pathos differently, using or dropping the cry 'Et tu, Brute?' And when the same situation recurs in a totally different context, with names and places changed, a character might die with a similar utterance on his lips. When writers engage in such playful deconstruction, the beauty of literature lies in the recognition, and perceived irony, that readers bring to the reading experience.

The capacity of minimal micro-fictions (sometimes referred to as 'flash fiction') to engage with plot at the risk of contrived motivation, or to delight in linguistic cleverness, even where action looks trivial, is of interest to postmodern writing that might otherwise grow wearisome if its purpose were only to expose the pretence of realism. Margaret Atwood's cycle *Happy Endings*, clocking in at about 1,000 words, contains six stories, each one headed by an alphabetical rubric (A–F), and the entire set is preceded by this premise and advice to the reader:

> John and Mary meet.
>
> What happens next?
>
> If you want a happy ending, try A.

Each of these is a separate story because each has a different ending (and all but A are distinctly unhappy, so the advice is accurate). Yet lengths vary, and while John and Mary appear in every story, they are not always the protagonists. In B, for instance, a certain Madge features and her involvement produces in the last line of C its own plot-line that means that the ending of the story is actually a beginning that leads into story D concerning Madge and Fred, of which we learn little because 'the rest of the story is about what caused the tidal wave and how they escape from it'. However minimal their story here, it is still fuller than that of the thousands who drown (no more is said). The story of Madge and Fred is, however, far shorter than the story of Mary and John in B, which moves from romance to suicide with bad sex in between in all of half a page. This story ends with the phrase 'everything continues as in A', a refrain that also occurs in other segments. But it is impossible to know precisely what this means, since 'everything' might refer to the sentences that referred to the marriage of John and Mary but now are transferred to Madge and Fred; or 'everything' might pick up with any of the other outcomes predicated of John and Mary from buying a house to retiring; or ‘everything’ might, as is most likely, exclusively mean ‘This is the end of the story’, which is the last line of A. How many concatenations it takes, as a mental exercise, to thin or thicken the plot is entirely left to the reader except in story F. There, the attitude of the authorial voiceover to the reader becomes quite pushy, in equal parts cajoling (‘If you think this is all too bourgeois…’) and fanciful (‘make John a revolutionary and Mary a counterespionage agent’), and is determined to control the endings because there can only be one authentic ending here, as in the opening story: ‘John and Mary die.’

John and Mary are no Heathcliff and Jane Eyre and were never conceived to live on in the imagination of readers like great novelistic heroines and heroes. Their hold on being lifelike at all is hardly more than syntactic, as subjects in sentences (John does this, Mary does that) with some psychology bolted on (Mary cries because she is abused by John). Is there a story to the story? Stories in which plot as action yields completely to the performance of language and the exercise of style might be thought to verge on a different genre like the prose poem; yet they cannot be disqualified as stories insofar as the representation of language is its own form of activity, and insofar as authors use the label deliberately.

What happens when figures with a previous life are transplanted into a fictional structure made up of segments can be experienced in Lydia Davis's *Ten Stories about Flaubert*, a cycle that starts serially and goes nowhere. Certain basic points of meaning and reference that might otherwise be the subject of educated guessing are determined by the title. Readers of Flaubert will have the inside track and recognize the Louis mentioned intermittently as his great school friend; they might well remember Flaubert as the wonderful correspondent whose great addressees were the same Louis and Flaubert's mistress Louise, who can be assumed to be the ‘you’ often invoked.

Unlike in Atwood's *Happy Endings*, these passages are unnumbered but each has a subject title, the sort of title you would give to a story, such as 'The Cook's Lesson' (no. 1) and 'After You Left' (no. 2). Without the titles, readers might think these were undated diary entries or letters. Paid-up Flaubertians will especially enjoy the pastiche, since Davis out-Flauberts Flaubert with perfect mimicry of his voice and style (not for nothing is she a distinguished translator). Each story has its own miniature plot, whether a story of a murder, a parting, a dental appointment, or a servant beset by a tapeworm. Because there are no dates, no sequence is mandated. Each piece is self-contained, yet adverbs like 'today', 'yesterday', and 'tomorrow' mark out time within episodes and possibly between segments. Depth emanates from the illusion of part and whole when arguably the sum is not greater than the parts and there is no whole. Atwood's story uses a playful variation of pattern because the entire conceit of the story is about subordinating truthfulness of content to a grammar of storytelling. How that outcome 'of they lived happily ever after' is achieved is not relevant. Like Atwood's story, the outcome of Davis's game is never shown to be in doubt because its reality operates according to premises as fabulous as those of Shalamov's Gulag are bafflingly inexorable.

Repetition, often *ad absurdum*, is the key pattern of such fictions. Serialism and serial criminality are natural partners. In her *Little Tales of Misogyny*, Patricia Highsmith, more celebrated for her novels, fused the postmodern theme-and-variation technique and the pathological violence of pulp. Each story is like a pearl strung on a single plot-line: 'they never lived happily at all'. Bad outcomes, especially for males, are par for the course. The effect of dread lies in anticipating when the metaphorical (and sometimes literal) axe will fall. That the terrible must happen is a foregone conclusion and just a question of timing. The balance between a deadpan tone and camp gruesomeness modulates between horror and comedy: in some cases, there is not long to wait, as in the opening of 'The Hand': 'A young man asked a father for his daughter's hand and received it in a box—her left hand.' In the story that evolves out of this terrible literalism the story itself plots to ensnare the young man.

The heroine of 'The Coquette' shuns a suitor and determines to rub him out. Her futile efforts take up two-thirds of the story. Once he realizes how wanton she actually is, he decides to join forces with another jilted suitor and turn the tables on her. They are brought before a local judge whose pity is inspired since he, too, was a victim of her coquetry. There is no moral to a story in which characters follow a playbook of decisions made only according to one binary choice: characters can only love or loathe Yvonne, and those who love her end up wanting to kill her. With amoral detachment, events corroborate the narrator's conclusion that there is perhaps nothing actually awful here because 'even Yvonne's family detested her'. In 'The Perfectionist', the druggy heroine has a mania for knitting, and the end is predicted in the title. Her salvation lies in a *reductio ad absurdum*: 'Knit, knit, knit. And what will Margot think of to do next?' We can supply that answer (when is a knitting needle not just a knitting needle?).

At comparable length, 'The Dancer' is more artful; it plots the movements of a dance and of a couple whose fatal misstep in the S-M game of temptation and teasing is predictable if not inevitable. Must things always get carried away? The married couple in 'The Evangelist' is set up for sympathy as an unsatisfied husband watches his wife become gripped by religion and divine frenzy: 'God came late to Diana Redfern—but He came.' Farce meets tragedy as we view her increasingly bizarre delusions and antics from her husband's viewpoint, culminating in her departure on a world tour as an evangelist. Yet the final line undercuts pathos with its ironic tone of detachment: 'Thus poor Diana met her earthly end.' In the world of this collection, there is no forgiveness and the delusional, the corrupt, and the insincere are punished not proportionately but absolutely and inexorably. If there is no justice, there is also no expectation of justice.

Plot-driven stories do not include dilated back-stories or get trapped in the elusive mesh of thought in the way that stories of consciousness do. How agents other than the protagonist, such as the state, fate, or stronger people, take over the plot is a preoccupation. In the existential drama that Sartre and Highsmith pursued, questions about conditionality such as 'what if' and 'if only' reflect the powerlessness of the subject to change fate. In the postmodern dismantling of reality, a few strokes of the pen, like fate, remake everything because the author unleashes language and structure as determinants. Even then, no story is entirely without plot. Perpetually intrigued by predictive approaches and random effects, Calvino delighted in showing the unanticipated consequences, often funny, that minuscule actions and deviations from norms could have on storylines. The separate episodes in the book *Difficult Loves* create a theme and variation sequence about sensual moments, often brought about by sublimely zany circumstances. What matters in the case of the besotted clerk, the opportunistic soldier on a train, or the woman at the beach whose bathing costume falls off is the initial frisson and the interior world of thought and fantasy into which each character escapes. Plot is not action and reaction. It is more alchemical, like the texture of skin on skin, water on skin, lips on lips, a heady and sensuous catalyst.

In suspenseful entertainments, the fabrication of a mystery and the guessing game are laid out for the reader. In fables of unreason, fate intervenes and relieves plot-driven suspense with its own unanticipated punchline—the twist does not necessarily have the same logic as in the classical detective story. In its postmodernist (and post-Holocaust) response to a world marked by religious and philosophical scepticism, writers like Donald Barthelme, Calvino, and even Don DeLillo have taken back control of their universes and not necessarily restored agency to their characters. This is the short story as delightful head-game and there is no fear about losing the plot.

Chapter 6
Ironies and reversals

The genre of the story has diversified away from plot-driven into character-driven works. The tradition of ironic reversal as the genre's defining feature still remains alive and well. It is indelibly associated with Guy de Maupassant. With his excellent sense of timing, Maupassant perfected the art of the short story as anticipation thwarted by shock reversal that he assumed his readers would find cathartic. His characters are reeled in on illusions and then, hooked by desire or avid for wealth, find themselves caught in a trap when malign fate intervenes. Relentless irony opens in the gap between what people want and what they get. An ironic twist, a reversal, a moral or psychological settlement round off the action and provide a satisfying sense of technical completeness and the pleasure of poetic justice or an irony of fate.

A backlash against this too symmetrical type of story set in early. Edith Wharton, an American who lived in France and set many of her eighty-six short stories on French themes, considered that his stories of marital intrigue went naturally with Gallic temperament and mores, marked by disenchantment, urbanity, social liberation, and a passionate nature. Elizabeth Bowen, putting her finger on qualities often mentioned, identifies Maupassant as 'an unliterary writer who is remarkably energetic, ruthless, nervous and plain'.

These qualities that shine darkly in Maupassant became hackneyed in the lesser hands of hundreds of magazine writers. Seán Ó Faoláin praised Maupassant as a 'relentless realist'. But the relentless effect has divided critical opinion for good and complex reasons. Frank O'Connor, while admiring his technical brilliance, also noted a fundamental lack of human sympathy out of tune with his view that comedy rules the human condition. Yet his influence is undeniable. It was said of Isaac Babel, one of the greatest Russian writers of stories, that 'his principal device was to speak in the same tone about the stars above and gonorrhoea'. He paid tribute to his French idol by making him the hero of his story 'Guy de Maupassant'. The story is full of the cruelty and despairing reversal worthy of his master, to be seen perhaps as the ultimate tribute or revenge. While the art of the short story has not abandoned Maupassant's technique, in general such a linear approach has become more the exception than rule. The art of the twist has more than one turn. Not every trap laid at the start must be sprung—sometimes reversals can be reversed or new ironies devised. And sometimes twists in the plot can come in the middle and even at the very beginning, only fully understood in retrospect.

The sting in the tail

Stories usually delay their twist until the very end. The sting-in-the-tail can take the form of a punchline, come-uppance, or tragedy. If a punchline is the aim, then stories can be stiletto-quick in flipping a situation into its opposite. Nella Larsen's compressed style illustrates the advantages of brevity. 'The Wrong Man' finds its society heroine newly wed at a glamorous party when she spies a man who holds the secret to her apparently tawdry past. Anxious to persuade him not to betray her secret and destroy her marriage, she sends a note and arranges a meeting with her supposed blackmailer in the shadows. Begging him to be kind and discreet, she pours out her worries only to realize too late when her interlocutor lights a cigarette that she has exposed herself to a total stranger. In the hands of ironists of the Maupassant persuasion, whether like Larsen or Hector Munro ('Saki'), such fictions certainly overengineer their endings for dramatic effect—but the pleasure comes in the anticipation.

Plot tension can also mount more stealthily. In Vladimir Nabokov's 'The Return of Chorb', time coils around itself like a double-helix. A pair of young lovers have eloped and, after one night in a seedy hotel, depart on their honeymoon in France. The bride dies of a sudden illness and the story catches the husband dolefully revisiting the immediate past by retracing their journey back to its point of origin to the hotel where they eloped. But the trip down memory lane is only one trajectory. It intersects with the fate of the girl's parents who have overcome their despair at their only child's misadventure and set off to find her. They arrive at the squalid hotel shortly after the bereaved husband returns to the room. Nabokov takes us up to the room, escalating the dramatic irony since only the reader can see the truth of the situation. The husband's resignation to his fate clashes with the revelation awaiting the parents—but their unimaginable reaction remains locked behind closed doors because the story ends before they learn the truth about their daughter. Is the author actually protecting the privacy of his characters or frustrating readers' catharsis?

Social comedy requires the satisfaction of revenge taken cold. Jane Gardam's 'The Tribute' is an excellent example of playful vindication. The story is to be savoured both for its satirical portrait of a group of elderly upper-class English ladies and the pace and deftness with which it plants clues in the seemingly empty chatter. Gardam opens with a chain of telephone calls relaying the information from Fanny Soane to Mabel Ince to Lady Benson that Dench 'was dead'.

> 'Who?' screamed Nelly Benson.
>
> 'Dench.'

'Dench?'

'Yes. Poor darling Denchie.'

'Thought she'd died years ago. Must have been a hundred.'

Mobilized to do the right thing for reasons of nostalgia and propriety rather than any deep feeling, the women, all formerly diplomatic wives, arrange a luncheon in London (as the cheapest expedient) in tribute, and the story manages its social comedy through further telephone calls, a letter, a car ride, and then finally the luncheon itself, this the last perhaps 'of a life-time of invitations—battlefields, of notes, menus, first and second guest lists, all professionally conceived, negotiated, carried through'. No matter the modesty of the tribute, the event arouses old organizational instincts as well as class hierarchies. Their fortunes reduced, their appearances run-down, these old-timers retain an invincible snobbery (the lunch is moved from Fortnum's to Harrods as 'less flashy') and class nuance is practically the only thing to which these otherwise nearly deaf and blind women gamely respond.

Assembled in the tea room, they digest the news that they are to be joined at the invitation of Lady Benson by a Miss Dench, a niece of their late nanny. Interwoven among their memories of Dench, mainly concerning her thrift and self-sacrifice, are their speculations about the niece, all in odd asides betraying unease because 'We were never primarily nieces.' 'Well, I dare say we'll spot a Niece Dench.' Further remarks dropped into their banter about Dench identify the virtue she made of being poor, disclosing that she never paid her tax toward the Old Age Pension; while another remembers an occasion when there were seven of them and only six eggs and one of the young children, a Polly Knox, offered to share her egg with Denchie (who as it happened refused). The trap has now been sprung. The longer they wait, the longer Gardam delays the entrance of the niece by piling on their meandering and not so hidden anxieties about their food: 'I don't see any point in spending money,' said Mabel, 'if the niece isn't here.' And that virtually ushers in their visitor. Dressed to the nines and glamorous from head to toe, their guest orders champagne with abandon as she celebrates the 'happy life of the dearest' Dench and proceeds to show her intimate knowledge of their lives and distributes 'trinkets', little mementos left to them by the deceased such as a tray, an elephant's foot (adapted as a boot scraper), and other 'little brass things', presents whose 'full horror' actually causes the old crones on nearly the final page of the story to rejoice in confirmation that their old nurse, as they suspected, had died in deepest poverty: 'To think that this sort of thing was all she had. All Denchie had.' And then it is that the guest turns into a deus ex machina and lets drop the bombshell: 'Well, except for the money,' says the niece. Poetic justice or tables turned, there is satisfaction in witnessing a game of harmless revenge played in small gestures and slights in which the underling trumps the spiteful.

Anita Desai's 'Diamond Dust' follows the linearity and pattern of cruel reversal that a late Maupassant or young Nabokov honed to perfection. Her story shares with Maupassant at least the premise of a senseless universe. For a writer of Desai's psychological insight, the blatant use of the structure must have compensating satisfaction in the effect of dramatic irony it allows. She even lays on the expectation of reversal thickly by appending the subtitle 'A Tragedy' and by using the very opening line to lay down the plot: '"That dog will kill me, kill me one day!" Mrs Das moaned.' The eponymous hero of the story is Diamond, the dog her husband acquired as a puppy. A senior civil servant of mature years, his attachment to his pet grows into a near-obsession, nearly blotting out family feeling: '"Not even about our own children, not even your first-born son, or your grandchildren, have you made so much of a fuss as of that dog," she had told him.'

To Mrs Das's repeated concerns about the animal are added the bemused observations of her husband's colleagues who, like a chorus in the background, comment sarcastically on the dog, which comes to be hated. Tension seeps from the story once it disappears. But this is clearly temporary, since Mrs Das cannot rid herself of anxiety, in the final pages more afraid that it will kill not her but her husband. It is no surprise, then, when Diamond reappears. At least initially, the dog is somewhat chastened and docile, but its diabolical nature bursts forth in an attack on the gasman when it runs amok and escapes. It is not long before a final tragedy strikes. The reader is not kept guessing for long. Mr Das catches sight of Diamond in the back of the dog-chaser's wagon (presumably the rounded-up strays are killed) and is killed not directly by Diamond but by a fall while in pursuit. His love for the pet has in no way been repaid: 'Diamond glittered like a dead coal, or a black star, in daylight's blaze.' There is no effect of catharsis to a plot of this kind because Mr Das is shown throughout as innocent of any malice, inexplicably besotted with an animal whose wild vigour is not an external prop to his ego, a virility symbol, or any other affectation. Is he punished because Diamond bit ankles and terrorized neighbours? There is no sense that he had it coming to him because the punishment does not fit the crime. In this universe, as in Maupassant's cruellest stories, there is more of an ineluctable sense of destiny fulfilled according to a law of symmetry that kicks in when characters are blind to the risk inherent in any excessive attachment, regardless of its positive or negative motivation.

Stories written with this kind of symmetrical reversal as their greatest effect raise questions about the ethics of reading. To what ends—didactic or aesthetic—do short stories represent agency, morality, criminality, and justice? Does cruel objectivity that is readable in fiction expose the reader's own inhumanity? Must the writer display sympathy? In the 20th century, writers like Saki, Somerset Maugham, Nabokov, Milan Kundera, Spark, all puppet masters controlling characters with a glint in their eye about wickedness, have proved adept at hiding the action of predetermined fate and delivering punchlines with dramatic power.

Fathers and sons: the irony of freedom

When Tobias Wolff says that 'conclusiveness inhabits the whole body of the story, not just the ending', he allows that characters who are fully drawn may also be more than dupes of fortune. In the hands of writers such as John McGahern and James Baldwin, the game may be rigged against characters, but they have more freedom to resist than Maupassant permits his characters. We find that stories grapple with a struggle between futility and agency. Both McGahern, in response to a strongly patriarchal and religious culture, and Baldwin, in response to segregation and bigotry, create characters who awaken to the clockwork of fate, pre-empting what might look inevitable.

The relationship between angrily remote fathers and obdurate sons, and between Northern Irish rural origins and urban flight, is McGahern's terrain, nowhere better seen than in 'Gold Watch'. Its main structural device is a counterpoint between accidental happenings that convey a sense of both free choice and oppressive determinist forces. It is an odd feature of 'Gold Watch' that while its ancillary characters are named, its two protagonists remain anonymously 'he' and 'she'. They are young, probably in their late twenties, and already acquainted from university. On the opening page they meet again when he is 'aimlessly strolling' down Grafton Street in Dublin. This 'lovely surprise' initiates a plot in which the gentrified couple struggle against the emotional force field of his tyrannical father, a farmer in Kilkenny and the owner of the gold watch. He cares little for the object because in the agricultural domain the seasons determine who works and when. By contrast, time is experiential to the lovers who feel that it is malleable and subjective. The hero, who narrates the story, is someone who has 'waited for love' as a graduate of the 'bitter school of my father'.

The father's idea of time, however, resists luck. That the father thinks himself as powerful as Father Time becomes clear when the couple journey to Kilkenny to see him and the hero's stepmother, Rose.

Three trips to the farm constitute the body of the story. In McGahern's families, frostiness is the usual reflex awaiting characters seeking to form their own family, and the 'disaster' represented in the first trip to the farm was anticipated from the start. What offends the female character is the father's observation, said 'out of hatred' in the son's view, that his fiancée looks close to 40. This is where the symbolic dimension of the gold watch signals the balance away from his domination of time to the son's control of his life. While the son loves the liberty that leads him to his beloved, he also obeys the inner compulsion to return to the farm to help clear the meadow and thresh the wheat. He makes a second trip and is given a warm greeting, changing into his labourer's duds and going at the haymaking zealously. At the end of the day, as he feels a satisfied exhaustion, he joins the older couple and it is when they are slumped in front of the television that Rose tips the gold watch out of the folded sheets she pulls out of the linen closet. She had put the watch there for safekeeping even though it had stopped telling time and was, so her husband had been told, beyond repair. He mocks her carelessness ('I'm sure you had it well planned. Give us this day our daily crash') but the fact that it is an accident aligns Rose with the life-giving motif of the unplanned.

When the son prepares to depart the next day, he takes the watch as his own. The value lies not in the gold since it has already been said that its quality was indifferent; rather, its value is psychological because the son had always assumed that it would one day come to him and, with it, a transfer of authority would also be effected: 'Then all weakness would be gone. I would possess its power.' A story about transfer is also about a reversal of power and fortune, and about time becoming unfrozen. If life is to blossom, it must move forward in time. On their wedding, the bride gives her husband his father's gold watch, repaired at very little cost. He does not wear it, treating it rather as a clock to be set on the mantelpiece. It is a sign of his youth and confidence that he finds a 'curious pleasure mixed with guilt to wind it and watch it run'.

In order to maintain tension, a balance must be kept between time as two forces, one of stasis, the other of change. At an airport shop on the way home from a trip, the son purchases a modern watch for his father. Calendar time is marked in the story by the progress of the seasons until the following summer, when the son, despite estrangement, returns yet again on his annual visit to the farm: 'I had come because it seemed less violent to come than to stay away, and I had the good new modern watch to hand over in place of the old gold.' Haymaking, however, is already finished, obviating the son's trip and eliminating the pretext for his visit. Nonetheless, the father, to whom the son lies about the gold watch, saying that it still doesn't work, expects the son to spend the usual two weeks. It is as though his marriage had never happened. The father's resistance to the passage of time becomes more pronounced in his hostility to the new modern watch, which he ends up smashing while breaking stones and leaving in the bottom of a barrel of poison. Can time ever be dissolved? Can the parts of a life ever be synchronized? The ticking of the new watch is muffled but persistent. What the son listens for in the silence of the night is some revelation, a moment of epiphany. None comes, yet there is the powerful philosophical realization of the present moment, of 'time that did not have to run to any conclusion'.

That sense of indeterminacy recalls the freedom of the story's opening. Aimless strolling at the end of the working week has changed into a more metaphysical sense of freedom, achieved when 'he' understands that life can be lived in the moment. The inevitability of circular time (the agricultural year) or time arrested (Father Time) has broken out into open-ended possibility. Having renovated the father's watch so that it tells objective time, the son does not need to wear it to have internalized the sense of time as an inner, subjective phenomenon.

A tragic story of wanton racial violence, James Baldwin's 1965 'Going to Meet the Man' represents brutal torture in all its revulsion. Any reader aware of the Jim Crow South will not expect the characters to escape their social conditions. The reversal of the expected outcome rests in Baldwin's decision to make the story's protagonist, a policeman called Jesse, both villain and victim because he, too, is shown to suffer from his abuses. And while palpably real rather than abstract, the story has the force of a parable in its demonstration that violence begets violence.

Almost the entire story is told as an interior monologue, a stream-of-consciousness of prejudices and obscenities on which Baldwin has imposed a tactful order. The man we meet in this story does not know himself. The great short story writer retains his humanity even as he exposes inhumanity. He burrows down into consciousness through dreamwork and unconscious language, however unsympathetic the character. Jesse thinks of himself as a good man, God-fearing, mostly indifferent yet given to lording it over 'niggers'. In a society built on racial domination, why would he think otherwise?

Tormented by impotence and exhausted by the racial tension flaring up around him, Jesse is gripped by the animal lust he feels for the black women he has sexually exploited. The reassertion of his virility at home is the challenge he faces. Is the cure of impotence to be found in surrendering the power that he wields viciously, or does psychological repair require an escalation of the violence that overexcites him? In the sleepless hours that follow from his failure to perform, partly during pillow talk with his wife, partly in the interiority of his own mind, he slips into memories. The story concertinas a recollection of that very day and one from childhood that must be the bedrock of both his racial prejudice and masculine identity. Jesse expects to find in remembered scenes of violence the titillation he needs to perform in bed when, in fact, they have unmanned him. That very day he savagely beat a young man. It is only at night as he remembers the way his victim called him 'white man' that he realizes that he knew the boy as a child. He is the grandson of an elderly client of his from his earlier days as a salesman. His savage reprisal against the grandson's defiance is shockingly drawn. He 'feels himself stiffen' when he applies the cattle prod. The cure for impotence is a matter of primal instinct inseparable from violence perpetrated against blacks, and that craving for violence is the thread that leads the plot from the present to the past. In the present, Jesse sees himself as a warrior fighting to defend civilization, increasingly embattled because a sense of shame that cannot be spoken has sapped his and his comrades' strength. Unease escalates as protesters sing through the night, and that sound triggers a memory of lines from a slave song, 'I stepped in the River at Jordan' (the song is 'Wade in the Water'). 'Where had he heard that song?' he wonders. The unconscious memory leads to an earlier episode. Another layer of meaning is peeled away in the title, for 'going to meet the man', its words, describes the lynching to which he was taken as a boy by his parents.

That day is the primordial point in his evolution from child to man, and the child of violence is its father, too. In contrast to the present unease, the memory embodies the effortless racial superiority his parents assumed as they drove to the lynching; in contrast to the present singing, the memory also carries an eerie silence that struck the child because unexplained; in contrast to the figure of Old Julia's grandson whom he tortured that very morning, memory provides some dialogue with a black friend, Otis, whom he played with, but who has now vanished because, like the rest of the black folk, he is hiding in fear; in contrast to the image of water in the song, there is the terrible spectacle of a pyre built for the burning alive of the lynched man. And, above all, in contrast to the present awareness of his sexual failure is the sharply etched memory of the castration of the victim even before his death. In his mind's eye, Jesse sees the man's penis, measures it as even larger than his own father's. That horrible image of emasculation proves the stimulus needed to revive his sex drive, and in the final lines of the story he whispers to Grace, 'Come on, sugar, I'm going to do you like a nigger, come on, sugar, and love me just like you'd love a nigger.' 'White man', as he is called earlier, needs to speak like a black man in order to recover his potency.

In a story steeped in a present full of paranoia about the breakdown of boundaries between enemies, the ultimate fear of racial transgression through sexual conquest implicates Jesse, who started out fantasizing about his experiences as a white man violating black women, in the act of falling into black speech patterns. Racism, so deeply ingrained from a moment of seemingly Freudian trauma, can only find its cure in a compensatory act that subverts the hierarchy that Jesse defends. His achievement of an erection (under a 'moon that has grown cold as ice') comes through what can only be total degradation, his moment of potency in fact a moment of impotence as a white man, possibly confirmed by the silent staring of his wife, who remains subjugated and mute. Few stories progress so remorselessly to a conclusion entirely the opposite of what their hero would want. In Baldwin's treatment, the precise calculation of crime and retribution transcends the pattern of reversal essential to a certain type of entertainment into an ironic study of how hatred rebounds on itself.

In plot-driven stories there is always a tension between inevitability and open-ended possibility. Endings are dominated by reversals of circumstance that look like poetic justice. McGahern's story delicately traces rites of passage in a young man's quest to shake off patriarchy, coordinating an emblem of time, the watch, with inner growth. Baldwin's story could have stopped before the hero's reckoning with his toxic masculinity. In plot-driven stories, then, an ironic twist, a reversal, a moral or psychological settlement round off the action and provide a satisfying sense of technical completeness and the pleasure of poetic justice, as in Gardam, or an irony of fate as in Desai. Yet in the hands of the best writers, the sense of inevitability does more than engineer a programmatic reversal: it creates a tragic solution by revealing an inability to change, as in Baldwin, or a happy, comic outcome, as in McGahern, or a set of circumstances that prove fatal, as in Desai. Reversals can be used to find a more humane, richer solution to a problem established at the start or to reveal the intractable nature of a flaw. In stories that have more than a binary settling of scores, irony can be more destabilizing than final.

Chapter 7
Chekhov's heirs

Dostoevsky is famously alleged to have said that all Russian writers 'came out of Gogol's "Overcoat"', one of his *Petersburg Tales*. Is it feasible to claim that the modern short story has come out of Chekhov's 'The Kiss'? In that story a hapless soldier, mistaken by an unknown lady for her lover in a secret assignation, gets the kiss intended for another. Feeling touched by grace and in a state of reverie, he strives to identify the owner of the anonymous pair of lips. The answer to the question about 'The Kiss' is 'yes' insofar as Chekhov's influence, particularly on the Anglo-American tradition of the short story, has been enormous. Beginning in the 1920s, and especially from the 1950s, a long line of short story writers, above all in America, Britain, and Ireland, have virtually self-identified as Chekhovians. The club has a wide and regional geographic dispersion. Asked to name a favourite collection of short stories, Edna O'Brien answered, 'Chekhov. Chekhov. Chekhov', and then produced a list of writers she saw as Chekhovian. In America, Eudora Welty, acclaimed with Flannery O'Connor as one of the greatest writers of her generation, is indelibly southern; Raymond Carver came out of the Iowa Writers' Workshop, while John Cheever's roots in New England somehow seem to echo the fading gentility of some of Chekhov's own heroes. The critic James Wood tartly noted that 'All you have to do nowadays is write a few half-decent stories and you are "our

Chekhov"', but then went on to proclaim that 'Alice Munro really is our Chekhov.' Welty thought that Chekhov was 'one of us' and her view that 'he is so close to today's world' is echoed in William Boyd's praise of his 'astonishing modernity'.

David Leavitt offers an insight into Chekhov's omnipresence. Until recently, he admits, Chekhov was a glaring gap in his literary education. Once he had read him he wrote, 'I felt as if I've been reading Chekhov all my life, which in a sense I had, since most of the writers I'd been reading all my life—everyone from Cynthia Ozick to Raymond Carver to Grace Paley—were reared on Chekhov.' As Tessa Hadley puts it, 'With Chekhov, the modern short story seems to spring into being fully formed, in all its ambivalence and sophistication and one might add in its balance of humour and futility.' The contention that Chekhov's influence can be felt even second-hand is not an article of religious faith and points to the perception that his craft, having opened a new direction in the art of the story, remains an ideal to be absorbed.

The cult of Chekhov

What principles, of storytelling and even humanity, does the Chekhovian signify? Social inclusiveness and open-endedness of form have been seen as part of his legacy. His material is drawn from the lives of ordinary people—and not only middle-class people but peasants, clerks, servants, theatre people, academics, wives, daughters, actresses—living through situations, sometimes trivial and sometimes tragic, that are often left unresolved. His skill in creating female characters from the inside out seems particularly remarkable after the one-dimensional portrayal of women to be found in Maupassant. A master of capturing with nuance what passes unspoken between people, he is also adroit in conveying the frustrations in human relations caused by all sorts of factors, including class, gender, and age. Chekhov's earliest stories were comic sketches, little more than elaborated anecdotes of sometimes no more than a page. His mature stories, written from about 1880, explore psychology and personality in relationships, in society, and sometimes in isolation and move well beyond comic gags. Characters are mercurial, their fluctuation of feeling created with remarkable plausibility.

Technically, there is no formula for writing a Chekhovian story. Yet the category has some meaning since Chekhov himself famously laid down strictures in letters to his brother as well as to his publisher, Aleksei Suvorin. He advises against 'lengthy verbiage', favours 'extreme brevity' and 'total objectivity'. These are qualities that all readers can see for themselves. What motivates them is a belief that the task of the storyteller is to deliver 'truthful descriptions of persons and objects'. William Boyd finds the source of the 'truthful', something beyond plausibility or verisimilitude, to be a 'moral disinterestedness' and 'clear-eyed analysis' that discourages overt moralizing or message-laden irony (as happens in Maupassant).

The other side of the coin from his supposed objectivity and emotional reserve or avoidance of moral judgement is a quality of Chekhovian empathy or pity that has increasingly come to be prized by readers as specifically Chekhovian (a feature of Edna O'Brien's writing singled out by John Banville). Chekhov's attentiveness to 'kindly' dreamers and indecisive characters should not be confused with soft-heartedness. While empathy is a type of restraint in not censuring foolishness and other character flaws, it can serve as the front man for the writer's pitiless perspicacity into the limitations and blinkeredness of characters. And it is the case that some Chekhovians do not equate empathy with benignity. Katherine Mansfield, also acclaimed for her Chekhovian spirit, complained that 'people on the whole understand Chekhov very little', meaning that they take him to be avuncular and fond when his effects may be more satirical or ironical. Taken together, the capacity for moral disinterestedness and empathy are the qualities that enabled Chekhov to excel in capturing the difficulty people have in saying what they mean or in saying the opposite of what they want to say.

Chekhov's stories are full of unfulfilled dreamers and therefore rich in ironies that usually remain latent, but once perceived show everything in a new light—at least to the reader if not to the personages themselves. Consider, as a quintessential example of Chekhov's stealthy manner, the example of the doctor Korolev (the surname derives from the Russian for 'king') in the 1883 story 'A Doctor's Visit'. Korolev is summoned to see a patient in the provinces, the daughter of a factory owner who is bedridden. He makes the journey, meets the girl, and has relatively little medical advice to give. Sleepless, he retires to the courtyard and has something like an epiphany in the night air. Against the din of the factory machinery he has a moral revelation about all the good he can do for humanity. Convinced of his own philanthropy, he remains buoyed up for the rest of the visit and departs, radiant with life and completely oblivious to the fact that he has done nothing at all for the patient. Chekhov has no need to intervene with a condemnation of his fatuousness or even a gentle hint of sarcasm. It is left to the reader to measure the gap between the scale of his vision and the reality of his therapy, and to consider how beguiled Korolev is by the first. More than the failure, what matters here is the degree of delusion that protects him from a true reckoning.

Situational irony of this kind is also critical to the Chekhovian story. It is used to reveal degrees of self-knowledge or obtuseness in characters who may be unaware of the gap between their ideals and their actions. Social embarrassment, character, delusion, and illusion can all present impediments to communication, and the three stories written by Chekhovians to be discussed here share that quality of theatricality, voice, and indirectness as characters make the necessary business of living, loving, and dying something about which talk can be refused, evaded, and sublimated into some other thing.

Chekhov as the hero of the Chekhovian story

Chekhovian writers unfailingly adore their idol and do not aim to beat him at his own game. But some of the most Chekhovian short stories are about Chekhov himself. What kind of story might he have written about his own death? Inevitably the answer is a story that finds the banal in the tragic. In this vein, there is no greater homage to the writer than Raymond Carver's pitch-perfect 'Errand'. The Chekhovian in his evocation—soundly researched though it is—can be found in a situation in which the comic curtails the sentimental, leaving all true feeling implied.

'Errand' opens on the name 'Chekhov' and the story's first third briskly moves forward in play-like scenes about his terminal decline from tuberculosis. They take in final farewells from his publisher Suvorin and Leo Tolstoy, a last visit by a German doctor, all supervised by his wife Olga. With a mastery worthy of Chekhov, often praised for his time-management of narrative, dates are noted and a newspaper report quoted ('Chekhov's days are numbered'). The background period of three weeks takes less than a page of prose. The countdown to a celebrated deathbed scene has begun. The errand of the title concerns the room-service waiter at Badenweiler, who brings the bottle of champagne and then returns to clear away the bottle and glasses. Chekhov was supposed to have drunk champagne before breathing his last. Carver brilliantly shifts attention away from Chekhov's ironical choice of bubbly as supreme unction. The minor event that upstages the tragedy of his death is the comic standoff between this young man (never named) and Olga. Unaware of the guest's identity and only dimly aware that he may be lying dead in the next room, he over-anxiously returns too soon. As he and the overwrought Olga face one another, she lost in thought, he in awkward silence, the story itself seems to perform an act of displacement from the grand to the trivial. The nearly mute scene between the two, which might take several minutes in clock time, requires four pages of social comedy observed with a Chekhovian sense of stage-worthy nuance (and the narrator, in the pathos of omniscience, adds a phrase to speculate that the waiter will most likely perish in the Great War).

Most Chekhovian of all may be the shift in viewpoint. 'She stayed with Chekhov until daybreak...' is how the final scene begins, and the narration continues with the Russian-sounding impersonal construction, 'It was then a knock sounded at the door.' Enter the waiter, and here Olga's perspective is subtly infiltrated. She expects the doctor. 'But, instead, it was the same blond young man, who'd brought the champagne a few hours earlier.' Objective and evaluative language blend tellingly: his 'trousers were also neatly pressed', and his jacket 'snug'; his cheeks were 'smooth shaven' and also plump; his 'hair was in place, and he appeared anxious to please'. His apology to Olga for the intrusion, couched mainly in small talk about restaurant arrangements, is summarized by the narrator, who then focalizes the view of the room, its untidiness, the location of the champagne glasses, the fact that 'a figure under the covers lay perfectly motionless and quiet' through the waiter who notices that 'the woman seemed distracted'.

Olga, a famous actress, is also now a widow in mourning, and the reader must wonder how the situation will be resolved. The longer she prolongs her silence, the greater his unease as he stands there holding a vase and nervously perspiring. How will she break the silence? Will the actress in her dramatize grief? Who can distinguish the gestures of a woman in a private drama from those of a great actress in a domestic tragedy? Her every gesture noted, his every fidget observed ('The young man touched his lips with his tongue'), Olga produces some banknotes, reveals that her husband has died, and asks him to find the most respected mortician in the city, worthy of a great artist. Keen to make sure the news is not leaked, she instructs him exactly on how he is to act in performing the errand ('not to become excited and run, or otherwise break his stride'), detailing not only his comportment but telling him, in the most descriptive pages of the story, how he will knock on the door, how he will hand over the roses to the mortician, and then how he will, only at the very end, disclose the name of the dead man.

Delivered quietly, 'almost confidentially', Olga's words could have been set off as a speech in a play, but Carver stays true to Chekhov's tendency to entrust interior speech and monologue to indirect reported speech, except at the very end, when she says, 'Everything is ready now. We're ready. Will you go?' And here, with an acute eye for the trivial thing that deflates all solemnity and also reveals character so prized as a Chekhovian feature, Carver puts the hotel servant in a dilemma. For that is exactly when, standing with the vase in his hand, he notices that, resting near the toe of his shoe, is the champagne cork. What should he do? To ignore it or to pick it up is a choice between the tender and the dutiful. While hardly a cliff-hanger, the gesture brings down the curtain on a brilliant vignette.

What we don't talk about when we talk about Chekhov

'Errand' belongs to the type of zero-plot story at which Chekhov excelled. Stories of this kind—Chekhov's 'The Kiss' is a good example—concentrate on a state of mind triggered by a small incident, and they are marked, as James Lasdun observes, 'by the pent energies of the situation' that 'disperse into an inconsequentiality that even today…feels shockingly true to life'. The tragedy, or comedy, has already happened before the story begins. The stand-off between Olga and the servant speaks volumes about the struggle between tact and duty each character faces internally. There are also stories in which tragedy looms just over the horizon, and the impossibility of talking about the dreadful draws characters into situations in which they must talk but cannot listen. Chekhovian characters, especially family members, are often more vocal when speaking past one another: they go through the motions of communication but fail to connect, their dialogue lapsing into insistent monologue.

This is the Chekhovian element in Grace Paley's 'A Conversation with my Father', in which conversation means a loving dispute between a writer-daughter and her elderly father about short story writing. Pitted against his traditionalism is her reluctance to satisfy expectations, especially for endings that tie things up. Writerly (and readerly) assumptions are put on the table; whether they are up for negotiation is the crux of their sparring. Now infirm and bedridden, the father asks his daughter to indulge him and write, perhaps for the last time, a story he would like, by which he means a story of the kind 'de Maupassant wrote, or Chekhov, the kind you used to write'. His criteria include the simple description of works in which there are recognizable characters to whom things happen in the right order, and the right order matters greatly to him, because the logic of the plot guarantees, in his view, plausibility and realism. The father is someone to be contended with: once a doctor, then an artist, he preaches the gospel of technique. Father and daughter then clash over how to handle plot: the linearity that pleases him in her view robs characters of choice. Orderly plots, she grants, deserve points for elegance but, 'Everyone, real or invented, deserves the open destiny of life.' Readers will perceive the irony of the situation in which the writer figure preaches openness to a dying man who insists on closure as the supreme virtue.

This artistic clash is the nucleus of a story in which the other thing that truly matters—his illness and death—cannot be talked about. Instead of arguing with her father, the daughter proceeds by trial and error, both capitulating to her critic and trying to re-educate him, while Paley herself must also have an eye on the reader. 'Pa, how about this?' precedes a first paragraph written as a concession that in her own view it is 'an unadorned and miserable tale'. It is not, in fact, what he had in mind, but this first version ('Once upon a time there was a woman and she had a son') will be the core tale out of which three further versions are elaborated.

Version one tells us that the mother and son are close, that they live in Manhattan, that he becomes a junkie out of boredom, she becomes a junkie to keep him company, and then he leaves out of disgust and 'we all visit her'. Between the present paraphrase of about fifty words and the actual story of one hundred not much information has been stripped out; it is quite threadbare, though adequately plotted. As a series of disappointments, it could not be crueller or more ironical than a story by Maupassant, who would have relished the irony in the contrast between the embedded story of family devotion between junkies concocted by the daughter and the main plot about the shared devotion of parent and child to the craft of the story. The father criticizes the story not because of its subject but because 'You left everything out. Turgenev wouldn't do that. Chekhov wouldn't do that.'

Clearly, plot in itself is not a sufficient condition for a good story, and something closer to Chekhov, the non-negotiable touchstone, must be supplied. Willing to start over, the daughter probes for a more precise sense of realistic detail, but the conversation quickly moves off appearances (hair colour, for instance) to questions of character. What the father misses is not greater description of appearances but rather a more acute eye for elements of a back-story, including emotional histories, that drive the logic of the story. She admits that in real life people might have time to 'run down to City Hall before they jump into bed' but not in her stories. This perplexes the father, and in her response the writer reworks the story we've just read according to his criteria, summing up as follows: 'Oh, Pa, this is a simple story about a smart woman who came to N.Y.C. full of interest love trust excitement very up to date, and about her son, what a hard time she had in this world. Married or not, it's of small consequence.'

The plot premise and conclusion of this story within Paley's story remain the same; however, the daughter has overloaded it with detail, much of it bizarre, aimed at establishing the identity of characters with a kind of hyper-realism. Every reader ought to be able to see that the result is a bad story. Even the dying father, ever the critic to the end and wary of her mockery, retorts, 'You have a nice sense of humour.' Her demonstration provides a masterclass in the dangers of starting with an idea of character rather than with a character, leading to silly distortions and unconvincing back-stories. And the daughter cannot even bring herself to complete this version and it breaks off abruptly with 'The End'. This parody of closure is once again part of the daughter's intention to show rather than tell her father how not to write. The parody of the fictional ending is also a displacement away from the impending separation of father and daughter about which neither can speak. An admirer of both Chekhov and Paley, the writer Ali Smith praises 'A Conversation with my Father' as 'profoundly, comically generous in its open-endedness', because it lets the energy of an infuriating relationship overwhelm the tragedy of its imminent end.

What is perhaps truly Chekhovian about Grace Paley's story is its frame narrative. The story is not postmodern or metatextual in the manner of Barthelme, for instance, because play with form is only secondary to its concern with human relations. Father and child cannot talk about his demise or their own relationship except insofar as what matters to them is deflected through their conversation about stories. That is the foundation on which their mutual respect is based; it is also the means by which they perpetuate the illusion, very much a sentiment to be found in Chekhov—although not only in Chekhov—that life continues in its familiar ways as long as it can. This is not a game of deception, but it does screen them from the painful consideration that their conversation will soon end.

A double irony

That the Chekhovian story also excels in exposing blind spots in self-knowledge, and sometimes cruelly so, may be what Mansfield intended in her comment about people understanding Chekhov very little. But the effect of that gap, between the impression characters make and their professed values, can be psychologically complex. While empathy certainly includes a tender awareness of human failing and childishness, it can also hide elements of spitefulness. Readers can turn to Frank O'Connor, one of the great writers of the short story, for many an example of a type of inhibition that looks Chekhovian, and this time not involving Chekhov himself.

The uses of self-deception are what amuses the narrator of 'A Bachelor's Story', who recounts the twists and turns of a futile courtship mounted by Archie Boland, an Irish civil servant and a former friend. 'Every old bachelor has a love story in him if only you can get at it' is a nicely epigrammatic note on which to start, and the emphasis on bachelors as a personality type might remind readers of Chekhov's 'The Man in a Case', about a bachelor of fixed provincial views. Archie grows smitten with Madge, a schoolteacher he meets on a trip to Connemara, and convinced of her genuine innocence, impressed that she was 'neither fast nor flighty', he believes himself in love although he never so much as holds her hand or makes love to her. Archie might gravely declare, 'I want you, Madge', but in the view of his friend this is 'magnificent but not love', because it captures Archie's complacent ease with standard phrases. In the eyes of the narrator, love can only sound genuine if it inspires a lover to exceed themselves.

The situation puts Archie to the test. Although he is certain that Madge is going to marry him, he has been blind to reality. She has, in fact, been seeing another man. Archie is described as 'one of those people who believe in being candid with everybody even at the risk of unpleasantness' and confronts Madge with the evidence. She admits that she has been stringing along several suitors and not choosing, because, in her experience, rejection only leads to their insisting or worse. ('"And I suppose you thought I'd commit suicide?" Archie asked incredulously.') Once she felt certain of her love for one of them, and she was tending to Archie, she declares, she would let the others down gently. The narrator, who criticizes Archie's candour by implication, sides with Madge, crediting her argument and telling Archie that this is simply how girls behave. To be sure, Archie is heavy-handed and pompous in denouncing her 'deceitful and dishonourable manner', but his conclusion that he can no longer trust her looks like a principled decision. The narrator, however, argues that 'she was simply telling the truth'. Not only does he laugh at Archie to his face but he confides to us that in thinking about Madge he finds himself 'falling in love with a woman from the mere description of her, as they do in the old romances, and it was an extraordinary feeling, as though there existed somewhere some pure essence of womanhood that one could savour outside the body'.

And this is where a particularly Chekhovian element is recognizable: is there another story here that has silently infiltrated the narrative? Archie confides his love interest to the narrator, wary that his friend might mock him from his own 'small experience'. But the narrator high-mindedly declares, 'I had no inclination to do so, for I knew the enchantment of the senses that people of chaste and lonely character feel in one another's company.' Scornful of Archie's old-fashioned gallantry (he doffs his hat to every woman he meets 'with a great sweeping gesture'), he is also scornful of bachelors: 'I never heard a bachelor yet who didn't take a modest pride in his own idealism.' It is only at the end of the story that he discloses that he, too, is a bachelor and silently smitten with Madge. Is the narrator, possibly a jealous rival, actually as charitable as he thinks?

The tone of the story has suggested that the narrator's approach is one of cajoling affection for a friend's inflexibility in playing the marriage game. There comes a point in the story, however, where Archie and the narrator row over what has happened. We have only one viewpoint on their relations. What if Archie feels aggrieved by his friend's insensitivity? Is a story told about one unsuccessful bachelor by another about bachelorhood or perhaps more about the teller of the tale? The relationship not talked about is between Archie and his friend. Writing the story about Archie has cost the narrator his friendship, something he makes clear at the beginning. Was his portrait benignly intended? There is something of a Chekhovian double bluff about how the men misread one another and the narrator's exposure of Archie and indirectness about himself. For all his cynical sexism, the narrator turns out to be a soppy romantic convinced that Madge has behaved like a 'nice girl' and has all the character Archie says she lacks. Although too frank with Archie, he clearly does not recant. For all his wisdom and his disdain of Archie, a bachelor he remains, ending up 'just as badly as Archie believed'.

V. S. Pritchett admired how the Chekhovian story, while consummately plotted, never gives the impression that resolutions are known beforehand, an observation that also applies to the best Chekhovians. The outcome of a story about Chekhov's death is a given, but the actual hero of 'Errand' faces a small choice; Paley's daughter and father refuse to compromise on art but will have to accept his mortality once the topic is exhausted; the possibly duplicitous friend of O'Connor's story may someday admit to himself that in mocking his friend he was covering up for his own insecurity with women—or not. All of these characters, in dealing with the circumstantial and emotional messiness of their own lives (what Welty called 'a sense of fate overtaking a way of life'), show empathy for their own and others' situation. As fates are kept off-balance, characters often face, or devise, ambivalent responses. Just as Chekhov's tragicomic irony can skewer failures of self-knowledge, his example of empathy can be put to the service of characters who themselves come to recognize their flaws—some change, others cannot.

Chapter 8
Endings

Isaac Bashevis Singer had a simple rule: 'I like that a story should be a story. That there should be a beginning and an end, and there should be some feeling of what will happen at the end.' His is a classic expectation that the endings of short stories symmetrically resolve the original germ of the plot. We read stories forward and expect endings to provide a certain conclusiveness to a course of action plotted from the beginning. Despite that expectation, major effects, such as poetic justice, comic relief, or tragic fulfilment, can seem to arrive out of nowhere, or from surprising quarters. The twist may or may not follow the logic to be found in the classic detective story. In Flannery O'Connor's 'Greenleaf', Mrs May, a widowed, landed lady, copes with tensions raised by her own penchant for morbidness, the maverick behaviour of her tenants (the Greenleaf family, whose matriarch has visions), her own son's emotional oddness, and a bull on the prowl lurking outside her garden. Any of these ominous elements could provide a shock ending—and when it does come it is the explosive description from different perspectives of the 'violent black streak' that delivers the *coup de grâce* one could see coming, yet not predict at all. A direct trail is not usually laid from the opening to the conclusion. The power of these effects lies in timing, false cues, complex causality. Reading and rereading carry different expectations: the rereader will bear the ending in mind, unlike the first-time reader who may second-guess the action. Yet the power of many of the finest short stories comes from the provisionality of conclusions that refuse to tie up loose ends and, on rereading, deliver more than ironic reversal by providing pleasure rather than a dominant effect of relief or plot catharsis.

Transition as its own end

Conclusiveness, therefore, may often mark short story endings but is not to be taken for granted. Stories, more than the novel, can leave dilemmas unresolved, lapsing into what the critic James Wood calls a 'leisurely enigma': the fluidity of personality and the open-endedness of the story seem commensurate in these instances. Stories can be true to life by observing how it is that despite what seems to have happened nothing has really changed. Here an anticlimactic conclusion provides the essential effect of a non-event story. Chekhov was famous for stories conceived with a 'zero ending': characters pass through experiences, only to return to their initial predicament largely unchanged. The tone of narrative voices often keeps the potential for different outcomes alive up until the end of a story, sometimes teetering between direct contradictions.

Childhood and growth, friendship and 'hateship' (as Alice Munro called it), infatuation and marriage are the moments in the life cycle and social existence that create stages for change as growth or release, and deterioration or disaster. Two stories by American writers capture characters ripe for change in youth and middle age, each dependent on some trigger to open their vistas to the wonder of perception. Sarah Orne Jewett's 'A White Heron' is in two parts; the resolution of the simple plot will be a matter of choice or instinct. A little girl named Sylvia is sent from the city home of her overburdened mother to live with her poor grandmother on a farm. The reticent Sylvia becomes the 'little wood-girl', at ease with nature. 'Afraid of folks', in the view of her grandmother, she is intuitively defensive of her habitat and is alarmed by the incursion of a naturalist. He is on the hunt for a white heron and hopes to employ Sylvia as a scout. She joins him, hoping to realize two secret dreams: to climb the tallest pine in the forest and glimpse the sea; and to save the white heron. In the account of her scaling the tree, nature has a near transcendent force: Sylvia's own bravery and tomboyish ease make her as much a creature of nature as the birds that twitter and the tree itself, which seems to lengthen. She *does* spy the heron, as the guest suspects, but she cannot be made to tell, and one has the strong sense that her purpose in seeing it was to fortify the strength of her silence.

It is hard not to think that Orne Jewett chose this bird because 'heron' and 'heroine' sound similar and here are close. But it is in the last two paragraphs that the story discloses much more fully the depths of Sylvia's inner life and the tension she feels between being a child of nature and a sociable being, loving the heron but also craving the moment when 'the great world for the first time puts out a hand to her'. 'She cannot tell the heron's secret and give its life away.' In the end, however, it is the cost of that 'dear loyalty' to the capacity for human love that prompts a question about choice. Both the girl and the naturalist preserve birds, but with opposite consequences. For the guest, hunting leads to forms of community and contact. For Sylvia, conservation leads to forlornness: 'Were the birds better friends than their hunter might have been—who can tell?' Nature owes her its affection, thinks the narrator, and must compensate her by bringing 'its gifts and graces' and telling 'secrets to this lonely country child'. Yet latent in the story is the stirring of the woman in the adolescent girl. There is a price to innocence and a price to the loss of innocence, and the choice between the two has only been deferred.

The end of Jewett's story is full of the promise of the growth of the child into adolescence. A story that moves in the opposite direction finds that wisdom does not necessarily come with age.

In John Cheever's 'The Country Husband', the sudden jolt of an accident proves life-changing because it seems to restore a state of innocence. Francis Weed's commuter flight from Minneapolis to the East Coast encounters heavy turbulence, and comes down in a field. 'Francis had been in heavy weather before, but he had never been shaken up so much' is the dry literal-cum-metaphorical report that prepares his reckoning with death. Although Francis lacks 'powers that would let him re-create a brush with death', Cheever can do the work for him in moving Francis physically from the macabre hilarity of the crash (during which the pilot sings, 'I've got sixpence, jolly, jolly sixpence. I've got six-pence to last me all my life…') back to his Dutch Colonial house in suburban New York, opening his eyes to how the ordinary cloaks the uncommon. Consider his neighbours' German housekeeper, a young woman known to have been publicly shamed for collaborating with the Nazis. Were the chances of her ending up in his vicinity greater than his chances of crashing? Local custom forbids the well-mannered of Shady Hill (perhaps 'shady' as in the 'shady wood' before the middle-aged narrator opening Dante's *Divine Comedy*) from mentioning the unpleasant as 'unseemly and impolite'. One does not speak of alcoholism and infidelity (touched on in the story) where everything must be arranged 'with more propriety even than in the Kingdom of Heaven'.

None of Francis's family pays much attention to his dramatic news. The air crash is his equivalent of Sylvia's tallest pine. Francis is awakening from death in life. His son and daughter are absorbed in their spat, his wife concerned to get dinner on the table. Playing off the material solidity of Cheever's realism are the slight intrusions of a new perspective. Sublimation into images and dream-language counters the prim repression of Francis's surroundings. The candles his wife lights are not just on the table, they are for the narrator and Francis 'in this vale of tears', as quoted from a Catholic prayer ('Hail Holy Queen, mother of mercy'). The impact of the crash seems to be sharpest on Francis's sense of hearing, now acutely sensitive and prone to translate sounds into emotions. His neighbour routinely practises ('nearly every night') Beethoven's Moonlight Sonata, and the sound wafts across the gardens. The lighting of the candles generates one subjective reaction; the sonata produces a more extended reaction culminating in a simile that encapsulates the feelings and fanciful yearning Francis invests in the piece, well beyond the suburban frame: 'The music rang up and down the street like an appeal for love, for tenderness, aimed at some lovely housemaid—some fresh-faced, homesick girl from Galway, looking at old snapshots in her third-floor room.' And so, when shortly thereafter the pet dog Jupiter barges in, we learn that he has the heavily 'collared dog's head that appears in heraldry, in tapestry, and that used to appear on umbrella handles and walking sticks'.

On every page some new vision of the unreal lifts Francis's vision of the real, thoughts coming to him on his commute, between the parking lot of the railway station and the platform. Spurred on by the 'miraculous physicalness of everything', he feels in 'a relationship to the world that was mysterious and enthralling', and sees through the train window 'an unclothed woman of exceptional beauty, combing her golden hair'. She passes like an apparition, but Francis, as though a character from *A Midsummer Night's Dream*, has one foot in a fairy-tale-like heightened realm of the senses. There is a suppressed Idealism or Romanticism to Francis, who, like a suburban American Transcendentalist, finds another realm of meaning on earth. The shock confirmed a sense that there is 'an abyss between his fantasy and the practical world', one that 'opened so wide that he felt it affected the muscles of his heart', and it cannot be repaired by religion or metaphysical thought. His manners loosened, his demeanour somewhat unhinged, Francis gets the attention he missed after the accident because his antics expose what is under the usual veneer of life. He leaves his wife, but then soon returns, and his single visit to a psychiatrist ends in slapstick rather than therapy.

The journey he undergoes is not from disaster back to normalcy, except that normalcy at the end of the story is resumed. Only in conclusion do we learn that the entire sequence of upsets, reversals, resolutions, and dissolutions has taken a week or ten days, and that the 'seven-fourteen has come and gone, and here and there dinner is finished and the dishes are in the dish-washing machine'. Out of the search for identity and certainty comes greater fluidity when the stable is dissolved by a sense of re-enchantment, when spiritual elation displaces church-going in a jazzy spoof of the self-seriousness of American Transcendentalism that is no less elated for that. Cheever's revelation teeters happily between comedy and impermanence. The promise here seems to be of the resumption of ordinary life in due course, perhaps slightly enhanced.

The modern story has the right scale and closeness to the individual to capture human subjectivity, from an adolescent girl to a middle-aged commuter. Stories that end with a glimpse of the future are only convincing if one can imagine a character's potential growth. We can see in a story by John Updike, Cheever's younger contemporary, famed as chronicler of middle-age and middle-class adultery, awareness of how easily the story characters tell themselves can fall into hackneyed epiphany. At Christmas-time, the newly divorced and soon-to-be remarried hero of his 'Domestic Life in America' pays a call on his ex-wife and children at their old home in the woods. He returns that evening to his interim life alone in Boston and sees on a walk toward Beacon Hill an 'electric sign' on which flashes 'in alternation remarkably, 12:00 and 0°. Fraser regretted that there was no one with him to help witness this miracle.' Updike knowingly parodies the use of epiphany as an automatic signal of profundity. This is not a hero whose dilemma matters very much, built as it is on the clichés of a midlife crisis. The plight of characters caught in true states of turmoil often end in uncertainty—not to be confused with the avoidance of an ending.

Unresolved contradiction

Readers of stories who are relaxed about irresolution will delight in the last-minute unbinding of what might have looked tied up. The open end allows for speculation. Examples of frustrated personal growth litter the pages of short stories, which have less of an obligation than the novel to tie up loose ends. *Dubliners* ensures its modernity as a collection by taking situations, rather than incidents, as the human predicaments of its characters. States of irresolvable contradiction pondered by a character with no available exit from a quandary leave the reader wondering—and never knowing—where things might eventually go in life and death. Like Joyce and D. H. Lawrence, Edna O'Brien is a stunning architect of the quietly implacable estrangement that drives couples apart. Of her many stories about misaligned couples, 'The Love Object' stands out for its remarkable intensity of feeling and wholeness of characterization, compressing into relatively few pages the anguish of a female heartbreak worthy of *Anna Karenina*.

The heroine, a television reporter, has let herself be seduced into an affair by an older, distinguished man. He, more than she, is the 'love object' of the title. The story is a retrospective take, by turns bitter and worshipful, on an affair that survives in the occasional meeting for lunch, full of estranged closeness: 'There were no barriers between us. We were strangers.' O'Brien is an unsparing artist of emotional tension, endowing her main character with perfect self-awareness ('It's how I fall in love,' she says on the first page) and neediness. We can see from the start what a smooth charmer her lover is, not only well groomed and impeccably mannered, but the master of 'an inner smile that came on and off' (a touch that is reminiscent of Tolstoy's description of Anna Karenina's own eroticism). Matched for sexual chemistry, their emotional needs are nevertheless asymmetrical: she worries about being made hungry for love ('an avaricious woman'), while he vows not to embark on a sordid affair, yet insists that the first signs of love spell the end. And so it does for him, since he makes the transition to flirtatious friendship seamlessly with a lunch here and a 'dear girl' there. The end of the story is, however, not the end of the emotional predicament in which the main character remains. The legacy of the relationship has been a heightened awareness of the world, which, even after it has ended, she refuses to relinquish. It is not necessarily that the everyday is now tinged with love and beauty. She observes nature, but also 'fresh spit upon the pavement' and in the faces of others she reads her own plight. Their meetings now refresh that awareness but have also opened a painful gap between the man as she knew him, the 'real he', and the present mere substitute. When they meet, he sometimes clasps his hands together as though in prayer when, in fact, she worships him and, above all, worships her love for him as emotionally compulsive. Surviving on meetings that nourish her dream of him and help her to bear daily life without him, aware that she is unloved, she remains trapped in a dependence on loving as its own object.

Closure as an open end

Is there no hope? This is the question in many stories, such as O'Brien's, that allow their characters wistful uncertainty rather than definitive closure. A lack of finality to an ending might also afford the excitement consistent with a well-plotted cliffhanger or, more philosophically, imply vast consequences that can never be told and might have remained latent in the story. Tobias Wolff noted that 'the besetting vice of most writers is a programmatic intention, making a story like an algebra equation with a solution at the end'. His story 'Hunters in the Snow' is both cliffhanger and meditation, coming close to that mathematical adding-up at the end; yet the sense of expectations fulfilled remains hauntingly off-kilter because of what remains untold. Where there is a hunting party the potential for violence is to be expected (and the title of the story might be a reference to Bruegel's great painting about three hunters, a canvas full of ill omens). But stories are not explanations, and readers may understand no better than the characters themselves why the element of personal chemistry in male friendship, generally tolerant of jibes, can sour violently. Where do things go wrong? The story opens in Spokane, Washington. Tub, as he is nicknamed, is kept waiting an hour by his friend Kenny, who has to pick him up as well as Frank, the third member of the party. An unknown driver stops, then races off at the sight of Tub's rifle. If this is foreshadowing, it is because a total stranger has picked up on a menacing vibe still hidden from the protagonists.

The real tone of menace is struck when Tub's ride does arrive, with Kenny at the wheel and Frank in the passenger seat, and the true group dynamic emerges. Tub feels threatened by the abrupt manner in which Kenny stops the truck, adding insult to injury by commenting on Tub's appearance. His nickname isn't random. After two frustrating seasons they hope for better hunting. Frank's role shifts, and he sometimes acts as a buffer between the two other men and sometimes has the last word ('"Tub," he said, "you haven't seen your own balls in ten years."') Under the casual shooting the breeze and on-the-road ego-pumping ('Frank breathed out. "Stop bitching, Tub. Get centered."') bullying machismo simmers. Kenny pulls a prank on Tub by driving away before he can get in the truck just to see him huff and puff. While Kenny visits a farmhouse to ask permission to hunt on the land, Tub appeals to Frank to try to mend fences ('I used to stick up for you'), confirmation of the uneasy group dynamic, further complicated by a subplot about Frank's girl and marriage troubles. Kenny's frustration at the poor hunting mounts, unassuaged by Frank's cryptic comment, caustically dismissed by Kenny as 'hippie bullshit', that the problem is not the deer, 'It's the hunting. There are all these forces out here and you just have to go with them.'

Within short order, the farmer's dog has been shot, as has Kenny, who lies wounded in the back of the truck; the forces out there use the forces within malevolently. Almost oblivious to their friend, the two others finally break through the crust of antagonism to talk about Tub's weight problem and Frank's love life, even stopping along the way to eat pancakes. Belatedly, they head for the hospital and the story winds to an end. Kenny is in dire straits. Lying uncovered in the tailgate because the blankets were 'doing him no good', he explains why he killed the dog. Wolff's omniscient narrator rounds off with the authority of an absolute voice that can alone dispense the cruel truth:

> Kenny lay with his arms folded over his stomach, moving his lips at the stars. Right overhead was the Big Dipper, and behind, hanging between Kenny's toes in the direction of the hospital, was the North Star, Pole Star, Help to Sailors. As the truck twisted through the gentle hills the star went back and forth between Kenny's boots, staying always in his sight. 'I'm going to the hospital,' Kenny said. But he was wrong. They had taken a different turn a long way back.

The narrator confirms what the reader works out: if the North Star is behind the truck then they are heading away from the hospital. Like the stars, as fixed points in the universe, moral law is a fixture that man by his very nature must know intuitively to be right. This is an ending without a concluding event. Readers will never know whether Kenny survives or dies, whether the two friends think twice about him or not—in short, what happens next. Does that matter? What explains the actions of the other two, who had seemed affable enough? Frank's line that there are 'forces out here' suggests a complete collapse of moral sense underlying an act of possible manslaughter. The final words—'They had taken a different turn a long way back'—extend the moral significance well beyond the plotline. How far back in relationships or in individuals' lives must one go to reach an explanation? The open end turns the story back on itself in the most searching way. Imponderables must be pondered about choices made and the relation of character, and character flaws, to ordinary morality. This is what we see here as well as in stories by

Shalamov, Sartre, and Kafka that are based on a tension between inevitability and the possibility of last-minute illogic. Stories that use plot to investigate states of mind, no less psychologically compelling than the novel, pit the search for logic against the chill of a world constructed according to inscrutable principles. Thematically, the stories treated here crystallize around the revelation or strife from which a life-changing moment can be imagined if not recounted. Where is the beginning of the end?

References

Preface

Alice Munro and Stefan Åsberg, *Alice Munro: In her Own Words*, The Nobel Prize, accessed 13 September 2020, <https://www.nobelprize.org/prizes/literature/2013/munro/25381-alice-munro-nobel-lecture-2013-2/>.

For recent discussions of storytelling as a biological imperative, see Brian Boyd, *On the Origin of Stories: Evolution, Cognition, and Fiction* (Cambridge, MA: Belknap Press, 2009); and Will Storr, *The Science of Storytelling* (London: William Collins, 2019), chapter 1.

For an example of internationalization, see David Miller, *That Glimpse of Truth* (London: Head of Zeus, 2017); writers are Spanish, German, Russian, English, French, American, Norwegian, Danish, Argentinian, Irish, Canadian, Indian, Australian, Pakistani.

For a systematic (if schematic) overview of the form and its structures and the history of critical approaches in English fiction, see Frank Myszor, *The Modern Short Stories* (Cambridge: Cambridge University Press, 2001). On how short is short, see, for example, Robert McCrum, 'On Short Stories', *The Observer* 21 June 1998, 85. For an example of a study devoted to the unitary thesis explanation of the short story—namely, every short story is organized according to a contrary duality so that nothing ever settles down—see Dan Jacobson, review of: John Bayley, *The Short Story: Henry James to Elizabeth Bowen* (Brighton: Harvester, 1988), in the *LRB* no. 10 (19 May 1988).

Frank O'Connor, *The Lonely Voice: A Study of the Short Story* (London: Macmillan, 1963).

H. A. Philips, *The Plot of the Short Story: An Exhaustive Study, Both Synthetical and Analytical, with Copious Examples, Making the Work a Practical Treatise* (Larchmont, NY: The Stanhope-Dodge Pub. Co, 1912).

Chapter 1: The rise of the short story

Primary sources used in the research for this chapter were sourced through a number of online resources: *British Library Newspapers* (<https://www.gale.com/intl/primary-sources/british-library-newspapers>); *The Listener Historical Archive* (<https://www.gale.com/intl/c/the-listener-historical-archive>); Nineteenth Century U.S. Newspapers (<https://www.gale.com/intl/c/19th-century-us-newspapers>); Nineteenth Century UK Periodicals (<https://www.gale.com/intl/primary-sources/19th-century-uk-periodicals>); *The Saturday Evening Post* (<https://www.saturdayeveningpost.com/issues/?issue-year=1821>); the *Times Literary Supplement Historical Archive* (<https://www.gale.com/intl/c/the-times-literary-supplement-historical-archive>); Ethnic American Newspapers from the Balch Collection, 1799–1971 (<https://www.readex.com/products/ethnic-american-newspapers-balch-collection-1799-1971>); African American Newspapers (series 1), 1827–1998 (<https://www.readex.com/products/african-american-newspapers-series-1-and-2-1827-1998>); American Periodicals (1740–1940) (<https://about.proquest.com/products-services/aps.html#overviewlinkSection>); *The Nation Magazine Archive* (<https://www.ebsco.com/products/magazine-archives/the-nation-magazine-archive>); *Harper's Magazine* (via <https://collections.library.cornell.edu/moa_new/index.html>); *The Atlantic Monthly Archive* (via <https://collections.library.cornell.edu/moa_new/index.html>); *The New Yorker* (<https://www.newyorker.com/archive>).

References

Quentin Reynolds, *The Fiction Factory* (New York: Random House, 1955).

Curtis Sittenfeld published in the *New York Times* a piece called 'Finally Write That Short Story' (18 July 2020: <https://www.nytimes.com/2020/07/18/at-home/coronavirus-fiction-writing.html?searchResultPosition=1>).

Chapter 2: Openings

Stories mentioned and discussed

John Kendrick Bang, 'Thurlow's Christmas Story' (1894) in *American Fantastic Tales: Terror and the Uncanny from Poe to the Pulps*, ed. Peter Straub (New York: Library of America, 2009).

Ann Beattie, the title story in her *The Burning House* (New York: Vintage, 1995).

Samuel Beckett, 'The Calmative' in his *First Love and Other Novellas*, ed. Gerry Dukes (London: Penguin, 2000).

Saul Bellow, '*The Old System*' in his *Collected Stories* (London: Viking, 2001).

Ray Bradbury, 'The April Witch' in *The Stories of Ray Bradbury* (New York: Knopf, 1980).

Raymond Chandler, 'Goldfish' in his *Collected Stories* (London: Everyman's Library, 2002).

Lydia Davis, 'The Busy Road', 'Almost Over: What's the Word', 'The Fish', 'My Husband and I', 'Her Damage', 'Kafka Cooks Dinner' in *The Collected Stories of Lydia Davis* (London: Penguin Books, 2013).

Fyodor Dostoevsky, the title story in his *Notes from the Underground, and the Gambler*, trans. Jane Kentish, ed. Malcolm Jones (Oxford: Oxford University Press, 2008).

Deborah Eisenberg, 'A Cautionary Tale' in *The Collected Stories of Deborah Eisenberg* (London: Picador, 2010).

Richard Ford, 'Communist' in his *Rock Springs: Stories* (New York: Atlantic Monthly, 1987).

Robert Howard, 'The Black Stone' in *Weird Tales* (November 1931) and his *Tales of the Cthulhu Mythos* (New York: Random House, 1998).

Etgar Keret, 'Upgrade', 'Joseph', both stories to be found in his *Suddenly, A Knock on the Door* (London: Vintage, 2013).

Stephen King, 'That Feeling, You Can Only Say what it is in French' in his *Everything's Eventual: 14 Dark Tales* (New York: Scribner, 2002).

Maurice Leblanc, *The Arrest of Arsène Lupin* (London: Newnes' Sixpenny Novels, 1903)

Katherine Mansfield, 'The Garden Party', 'Bains Turcs' in her *Selected Stories*, ed. Vincent O'Sullivan (New York: W. W. Norton, 2006).

Lorrie Moore, 'Wings' in her *Bark* (New York: Knopf, 2014).

Alice Munro, the title story in her *Hateship, Friendship, Courtship, Loveship, Marriage: Stories* (New York: Alfred A. Knopf, 2001).
E. Philips Oppenheim, *The Great Impersonation* (London: A. L. Burt Company with Little Brown & Co., 1920).
William Trevor, 'Afternoon Dancing' in his *Collected Stories* (London: Penguin, 1992).
David Foster Wallace, 'Good Old Neon' in his *Oblivion: Stories* (London: Abacus, 2010).
Eudora Welty, 'Looking at Short Stories' in her *The Eye of the Story: Selected Essays and Reviews* (New York: Random House, 1978).
Joy Williams, 'Hammer' in her *The Visiting Privilege* (London: Tuskar Rock Press, 2015).

References

Oxford Dictionary of Literary Terms, 4th edn, ed. Chris Baldick (Oxford: Oxford University Press, 2015).

Chapter 3: Voices

Stories mentioned and discussed

James Baldwin, 'Sonny's Blues' in his *Going to Meet the Man* (New York: Dial Press, 1965).
Fyodor Dostoevsky, 'Bobok' in his *The Crocodile and Other Stories*, trans. Constance Garnett and Preface by James Wood (London: Riverrun Books, 2019).
Gabriel García Márquez, 'The Other Side of Death' in his *Collected Stories*, trans. Gregory Rabassa and J. S. Bernstein (London: Penguin Books, 1991).
Helen Garner, 'The Life of Art' in her *My Hard Heart: Selected Fiction* (London: Penguin, 2004).
Edward P. Jones, *In the Blink of God's Eye* (New York: Amistad Press, 2006).
James Joyce, *Dubliners: Centennial Edition* (New York: Penguin, 2014).
Jamaica Kincaid, 'Girl' in her *At the Bottom of the River* (New York: Farrar, Straus and Giroux, 1983).
Bernard Malamud, 'The Magic Barrel' in his *The Magic Barrel and Other Stories* (New York: Farrar, Straus and Giroux, 2003).
Lorrie Moore, *'Two Boys'* in her *Like Life* (New York: Alfred Knopf, 1990).
Alice Munro, 'Pride' in her *Dear Life: Stories* (New York: Vintage, 2013).

George Saunders, 'Victory Lap' in his *Tenth of December* (London: Bloomsbury, 2013).
Leo Tolstoy, 'Kholstomer: A Story of a Horse' [sometimes translated as 'Strider'] in his *The Devil and Other Stories*, trans. Louise and Aylmer Maude, ed. Richard F. Gustafson (Oxford: Oxford University Press, 2009).
Richard Yates, 'The Best of Everything' in *The Collected Stories of Richard Yates* (New York: Picador, 2002).

References

Dorothea Brande, *Becoming a Writer* (New York: Harcourt, Brace, 1934; much reprinted).

Chapter 4: Place

Stories mentioned and discussed

Richard Ford, 'Occidentals' in his *Women with Men* (New York: Knopf, 1997).
Mavis Gallant, 'Speck's Idea' in *The Selected Stories of Mavis Gallant* (London: Bloomsbury, 2004).
Henry James, 'Madame de Mauves' in *The Complete Tales of Henry James*, ed. Leon Edel, vol. 3: 1898–1899 (London: Rupert Hart-Davis, 1964).
Bernard Malamud, *Pictures of Fidelman* (New York: Farrar, Straus & Giroux, 1969).
Katherine Mansfield, 'Je ne parle pas français' and 'Marriage à la Mode' in her *Selected Stories*, ed. Vincent O'Sullivan (New York: W. W. Norton, 2006).
Guy de Maupassant, 'A Parisian Adventure' ['A Parisian Affair'] in his *A Parisian Affair and Other Stories*, trans. and ed. Sian Miles (London: Penguin, 2004).
Georges Perec, 'The Runaway' in *Paris Tales*, ed. Helen Constantine (Oxford: Oxford University Press, 2004).
Edgar Allan Poe's 1849 trilogy, 'The Murders in the Rue Morgue', 'The Mystery of Marie Roget', and 'The Purloined Letter' in his *The Complete Stories* (London: Everyman Classics, 1993).
John Steinbeck, *The Pastures of Heaven* (New York: Penguin, 1995).
Ivan Turgenev, *A Sportman's Notebook*, trans. Charles and Natasha Hepburn (London: Everyman's Classics, 1992).
Eudora Welty, *The Golden Apples* (New York: Harcourt, Brace, 1949).

Edith Wharton, 'The Last Asset' in her *Collected Stories, 1891–1910* (New York: Library of America, 2001).

Chapter 5: The plot thickens… and thins

Stories mentioned and discussed

Ryunosuke Akutagawa, 'In a Bamboo Grove' in his *Rashomon and Seventeen Other Stories*, trans. Jay Rubin et al. (London: Penguin, 2009).

Margaret Atwood, 'Happy Endings' in her *Murder in the Dark* (Toronto: Coach House Books, 1983).

Jorge Luis Borges, 'The Plot' ['La Trama'] in his *Dreamtigers*, trans. Mildred Boyer and Harold Morland (Austin, Tex.: University of Texas Press, 1985).

Italo Calvino, *Difficult Loves*, trans. William Weaver (London: Vintage Books, 1999).

Lydia Davis, 'Ten Stories about Flaubert' in *The Paris Review* 194 (Fall 2010).

Hammett's Continental Op stories in Dashiell Hammett, *Crime Stories & Other Writings*, ed. Steven Marcus (New York: Library of America, 2013).

Patricia Highsmith, *Little Tales of Misogyny* (London: Virago, 2015).

Henry James, The Turn of the Screw in *The Complete Tales of Henry James*, ed. Leon Edel, vol. 3: 1873–1875 (London: Rupert Hart-Davis, 1962).

Edward P. Jones, *All Aunt Hagar's Children: Stories* (New York: Amistad, 2007).

Franz Kafka, 'A Country Doctor' in his *Metamorphosis and Other Stories*, trans. Michael Hofmann (London: Penguin, 2019).

Guy de Maupassant, 'The Necklace' in *Guy de Maupassant's Selected Works*, trans. Sandra Smith, ed. Robert Lethbridge (New York: W. W. Norton, 2016).

Alice Munro, the title story in her *The Love of a Good Woman* (London: Vintage, 2000).

Edgar Allan Poe, 'Cask of Amontillado' in his *The Complete Stories* (London: Everyman's Library Classics, 1992).

Jean-Paul Sartre, *The Wall*, trans. Andrew Brown (London: Calder Publications, 2018).

Varlam Shalamov, 'The Lawyers' Conspiracy' in his *Kolyma Stories*, trans. Donald Rayfield (New York: New York Review of Books, 2018).

Elizabeth Taylor, 'Fly Paper' in her *Complete Short Stories* (London: Virago, 2012).

Eudora Welty, 'Why I Live at the P.O.' in *Selected Stories of Eudora Welty: A Curtain of Green and Other Stories*, introd. Katherine Ann Porter (San Diego: Harvest Books: 1979).

References

John Updike, <https://www.youtube.com/watch?v=s-G5bH7axag>

Chapter 6: Ironies and reversals

Stories mentioned and discussed

Isaac Babel, 'Guy de Maupassant' in The Complete Works of Isaac Babel, trans. Peter Constantine, ed. Nathalie Babel (New York: W. W. Norton, 2001).

James Baldwin, the title story in his collection *Going to Meet the Man* (New York: Dial Press, 1965).

Elizabeth Bowen, 'Review. *Faber Book of Modern Short Stories*' (1936) republished in *Collected Impressions* (London: Longmans Green, 1950), p. 39.

Anita Desai, 'Diamond Dust: A Tragedy' in her *The Complete Stories* (London: Vintage Classics, 2018).

Jane Gardam, 'The Tribute' in *The Stories of Jane Gardam* (New York: Europa Editions, 2014).

Nella Larsen, 'The Wrong Man' in *The Complete Fiction of Nella Larsen* (New York: Random House, 2001).

John McGahern, 'Gold Watch' in his *The Collected Stories* (London: Faber and Faber, 2014).

Vladimir Nabokov, 'The Return of Chorb' in his *Collected Stories* (London: Penguin, 2001).

Edith Wharton, *French Ways and their Meaning* (London: D. Appleton & Co, 1919).

Chapter 7: Chekhov's heirs

Stories mentioned and discussed

Raymond Carver, 'Errand' in his *Where I'm Calling From: Selected Stories* (New York: Atlantic Monthly, 1991).

Anton Chekhov, *The Kiss and Other Stories*, trans. Hugh Aplin (London: Alma Classics, 2016).

Anton Chekhov, 'A Case History' ['A Doctor's Visit'] in his *Selected Stories*, ed. Cathy Popkin (New York: W. W. Norton, 2014).
Nikolai Gogol, 'Petersburg Tales' in his *Plays and Petersburg Tales*, trans. Christopher English and ed. Richard Peace (Oxford: Oxford University Press, 2008).
Frank O'Connor, 'A Bachelor's Story' in his *Collected Stories* (New York: Random House, 1990).
Grace Paley, 'A Conversation with my Father' in Grace Paley, *The Collected Stories* (New York: Farrar, Straus and Giroux, 1994).

References

John Banville, 'Edna O'Brien, Informed by Chekhov, Inspired by Vulnerability', *The Irish Times*, 23 Nov. 2013.
Julian Barnes, 'On "Ireland's Chekhov": Frank O'Connor', *The Guardian*, 2 July 2005.
William Boyd, 'A Chekhov Lexicon', *The Guardian*, 3 July 2004, p. 26.
William Boyd, 'Anton Chekhov: A Lifetime of Lovers', *The Guardian*, 1 Mar. 2013.
Evgeniia Butenina, 'Raymond Carver as "The American Chekhov"', *Journal of Siberian Federal University*, Nov. 2018, pp. 27–33.
Tessa Hadley, 'Top 10 Short Stories', *The Guardian*, 11 Sept. 2013 (she chose 'Ward 6').
James Lasdun, 'The Wonder of Chekhov', *The Guardian*, 6 Feb. 2010.
David Leavitt, 'By the Book', *The New York Times*, 26 June 2014.
Katherine Mansfield, as cited in *The Observer*, 18 May 1924, p. 9.
G. R. Noyes, 'Chekhov', *The Nation* 107 (10 Dec. 1918), p. 406.
Edna O'Brien, 'By the Book', *The New York Times*, 21 May 2015.
V. S. Pritchett, 'Katherine Mansfield's Short Stories', *The Listener* 912 (4 July 1946).
Ali Smith, 'Ali Smith Reads Grace Paley', *The Guardian* UK Culture Podcast, 21 Dec. 2010.
Eudora Welty, 'The Art of Fiction No. 47', *The Paris Review* 55 (Fall 1972).
James Wood, 'An English Chekhov: V. S. Pritchett and the Condescension of Posterity', *TLS*, 4 Jan. 2002, pp. 12–13. James Wood, 'Alice Munro, our Chekhov', *The New Yorker*, 10 Oct. 2013.

Chapter 8: Endings

Stories mentioned and discussed

John Cheever, 'The Country Husband' in his *The Stories of John Cheever* (New York: Knopf, 1978).

Sarah Orne Jewett, 'A White Heron' in her *Novels and Stories*, ed. Michael Davitt Bell (New York: Library of America, 1994).

Edna O'Brien, 'The Love Object' in her *The Love Object: Selected Stories* (London: Faber & Faber, 2013).

Flannery O'Connor, 'Greenleaf' in her *Everything that Rises Must Converge* (New York: Farrar, Straus and Giroux, 1965).

John Updike, 'Domestic Life in America' in his *Collected Later Stories*, ed. Christopher Carduff (New York: Library of America, 2013).

Tobias Wolff, 'Hunters in the Snow' in his *Our Story Begins:* New and Selected Stories (New York: Alfred Knopf, 2008).

References

Isaac Bashevis Singer, 'The Art of Fiction No. 42', *The Paris Review* 44 (Fall 1968).

James Wood, with reference to Edith Pearlman, 'Look Again', *The New Yorker*, 16 Feb. 2015.

Further reading

Some suggestions of further stories with a noteworthy treatment of this aspect of form are given below.

Chapter 2: Openings

Angela Carter, 'The Courtship of Mr Lyon' in her *The Bloody Chamber and Other Stories* (London: Penguin, 2015).

M. R. James, 'The Stalls of Barchester Cathedral' in his *More Ghost Stories of an Antiquary* (London: Edward Arnold, 1910).

D. H. Lawrence, 'The Horse Dealer's Daughter', 'New Eve and Old Adam' in his *Collected Stories* (London: Everyman Classics, 2012).

Carson McCullers, 'Who has Seen the Wind?' in her *The Mortgaged Heart* (London: Penguin, 1975).

Alice Munro, 'Pride' in *Dear Life* (London: Chatto & Windus, 2012).

Viet Thanh Nguyen, 'War Years' in his *The Refugees* (New York: Grove Press, 2017).

V. S. Pritchett, 'The Camberwell Beauty' in his *Complete Collected Stories* (New York: Vintage Books, 1992).

Chapter 3: Voices

Donald Barthelme, 'The Genius' in his *Forty Stories*, introd. Dave Eggers (New York: Penguin Books, 2005).

Anne Enright, 'Until the Girl Died' in her *Taking Pictures* (London: Jonathan Cape, 2008).

Henry Green, 'The Lull' in *The Penguin Book of the British Short Story*, vol. 2: *From P. G. Wodehouse to Zadie Smith*, ed. Philip Hensher (London: Penguin Classics, 2015).

Amy Hempel, 'Tonight is a Favor to Holly' in Amy Hempel, *The Collected Stories* (New York: Scribner, 2006).

Carson McCullers, 'Wunderkind' in her *The Mortgaged Heart* (Harmondsworth: Penguin Modern Classics, 1978).

Margaret Oliphant, 'The Library Window' in *The Penguin Book of the British Short Story*, vol. 1: *From Daniel Defoe to John Buchan*, ed. Philip Hensher (London: Penguin Classics, 2015).

Alan Sillitoe, 'Mimic' in *The Penguin Book of the British Short Story*, ed. Hensher, vol. 2.

Muriel Spark, 'Bang Bang, you're Dead' in her *The Complete Short Stories* (Edinburgh: Canongate, 2011).

Eudora Welty, 'Where Is the Voice Coming From? in *The Collected Stories of Eudora Welty* (London: Marion Boyars, 1981).

Chapter 4: Place

Joseph Conrad, 'Outpost of Progress' in his *Tales of Unrest* (London: Alma Classics, 2018).

Helen Garner, 'In Paris' in *Postcards from Surfers: Stories* (Fitzroy, Victoria: McPhee Gribble, 1985).

D. H. Lawrence, 'Daughters of the Vicar' in his *Collected Stories* (London: Everyman Classics, 2012).

Doris Lessing, 'The DeWets Come to Kloof Grange' in *The Secret Self: Short Stories by Women*, ed. Hermione Lee (London: J. M. Dent & Sons, 1985).

Prosper Mérimée, 'Matteo Falcone' in his *Carmen and Other Stories* (Oxford: Oxford University Press, 1989).

Chapter 5: The plot thickens . . . and thins

Joseph Conrad, 'The Tale' in *50 Great Short Stories*, ed. Milton Crane (New York: Bantam Classic, 2005).

Julio Cortazar, 'Axolotl', 'The Distance', 'A Yellow Flower' in his *Blow-Up and Other Stories*, trans. Paul Blackburn (New York: Pantheon Books, 1985).

Clarice Lispector, 'The Fifth Story' in her *The Complete Stories*, trans. Katrina Dodson, ed. Benjamin Moser (New York: New Directions, 2018).

Gabriel García Márquez, 'Tuesday Siesta', 'One Day After Saturday' in his *Collected Stories*, trans. Gregory Rabassa and J. S. Bernstein (London: Penguin Books, 1991).
George Saunders, 'Home' in his *Tenth of December* (London: Bloomsbury, 2013).

Chapter 6: Ironies and reversals

Donald Antrim, 'Another Manhattan' in his *The Emerald Light in the Air* (London: Granta, 2014).
Roddy Doyle, 'The Pram' in *The Granta Book of the Irish Short Story* (London: Granta, 2010).
Nadine Gordimer, 'Happy Event' in her *Selected Stories* (New York: The Viking Press, 1976).
Robert Stone, 'Helping' in *100 Years of the Best American Short Stories*, ed. Lorrie Mooreand Heidi Pitlor (Boston: Houghton Mifflin Harcourt, 2015).
Elizabeth Taylor, 'In and Out the Houses' in her *Complete Short Stories* (London: Virago, 2012).
Sylvia Townsend Warner, 'The Trumpet Shall Sound' in her *A Garland of Straw* (London: Chatto & Windus, 1943).

Chapter 7: Chekhov's heirs

Aldo Buzzi, 'Chekhov in Sondrio', *The New Yorker*, 6 Sept. 1992.
Richard Ford, 'The Womanizer' in his *Women with Men: Three Stories* (New York: Alfred A. Knopf, 1997).
John McGahern, 'The Beginning of an Idea' in his *The Collected Stories* (London: Faber and Faber, 2014).

Chapter 8: Endings

Claire-Louise Bennett, 'Once the Sun Has Run its Course' in *The White Review* 20 (June 2017).
J. D. Salinger, 'A Perfect Day for Bananafish' in his *For Esme—with Love and Squalor* (London: Penguin Books, 1981).
Leonardo Sciascia, 'The Long Voyage' in *The Penguin Book of Italian Short Stories*, ed. Jhumpa Lahiri (London: Penguin Classics, 2019).

I. B. Singer, the title story in *A Friend of Kafka* (New York: Farrar, Straus & Giroux, 1970).
William Trevor, 'The Hill Bachelors' in his *Selected Stories* (London: Penguin Books, 2011).

Anthologies of short stories

Richard Bausch, ed., *The Norton Anthology of Short Fiction*, 8th edn (New York: W. W. Norton, 2015).
A. S. Byatt, ed., *The Oxford Book of English Short Stories* (Oxford: Oxford University Press, 2009).
Robert Chandler, ed., *Russian Short Stories from Pushkin to Buida* (London: Penguin, 2005).
Martin Edwards, ed., *Crimson Snow: Winter Mysteries* (London: The British Library, 2016).
Anne Enright, ed., *The Granta Book of the Irish Short Story* (London: Granta, 2010).
Richard Ford, ed., *The Granta Book of the American Long Story* (London: Granta, 1999).
Richard Ford, ed., *The Granta Book of the American Short Story*, 2 vols. (London: Granta, 2008).
Sarah Gilmartin and Declan Meade, eds, *Stinging Fly Stories* (Dublin: Stinging Fly Press, 2019).
Philip Hensher, ed., *The Penguin Book of the British Short Story*, 2 vols. (London: Penguin Books, 2015).
Bryan Karetnyk, ed., *Russian Émigré Short Stories from Bunin to Yanovsky* (London: Penguin Classics, 2018).
Laurie R. King and Leslie S. Klinger, ed., *Echoes of Sherlock Holmes* (New York: Pegasus Crime, 2016).
Jhumpa Lahiri, ed., *The Penguin Book of Italian Short Stories* (London: Penguin Classics, 2019).
Hermione Lee, ed., *The Secret Self: Short Stories by Women*, 2 vols. (London: J. M. Dent & Sons, 1985).
David Marcus, ed., *Irish Ghost Stories* (London: Bloomsbury, 1999).
Lorrie Moore and Heidi Pitlor, eds, *100 Years of the Best American Short Stories* (Boston and New York: Houghton Mifflin, 2015).
Jay Rubin, ed., *The Penguin Book of Japanese Short Stories* (London: Penguin Classics, 2019).
Elaine Showalter, ed., *Scribbling Women: Short Stories by Nineteenth-Century American Women* (London: J. M. Dent, 1997).

John Updike and Katrina Kenison, eds, *The Best American Short Stories of the Century* (Boston and New York: Houghton Mifflin, 1999).

Historic manuals and handbooks

Charles Raymond Barrett, *Short Story Writing: A Practical Treatise on the Art of the Short Story* (New York: Baker and Taylor Company, 1898).

N. Bryllion Fagin,*Short-Story Writing: An Art or a Trade?* (New York: Thomas Seltzer, 1923).

Elias Lieberman, *The American Short Story: A Study of the Influence of Locality in its Development* (Ridgewood, NJ: The Editor, 1912).

Edward J. O'Brien, *The Advance of the American Short Story* (New York: Dodd, Mead and Company, 1931).

H. A. Philips, *The Plot of the Short Story: An Exhaustive Study, Both Synthetical and Analytical, with Copious Examples, Making the Work a Practical Treatise* (Larchmont: Stanhope-Dodge Publishing Company, 1912).

Walter Pitkin, *How to Write Stories* (New York: Harcourt, Brace and Company, 1923).

James G. Watson, 'The American Short Story: 1930–1945' in *The American Short Story, 1900–1945: A Critical History*, ed. Philip Stevick (Boston: Twayne Publishers, 1984), pp. 103–47.

General further reading

Jean-Pierre Aubrit, *Le Conte et la nouvelle* (Paris: A. Colin, 1997).

Tom Bailey, *A Short Story Writer's Companion* (New York and Oxford: Oxford University Press, 2001).

Jacqueline Bardolph, ed., *Telling Stories: Postcolonial Short Fiction in English* (Amsterdam: Rodopi, 2001).

Julian Barnes, *On We Sail* [Review of: Guy de Maupassant, *Afloat*], *LRB* 31, no. 21 (2009), pp. 25–8.

B. Eikhenbaum, 'O. Henry and the Theory of the Short Story' [1925], in *Readings in Russian Poetics*, ed. L. Matejka and K. Pomorska (Cambridge, Mass.: MIT Press, 1971), pp. 227–70.

Lucy Evans, Emma Smith, and Mark McWatt, eds, *The Caribbean Short Story: Critical Perspectives* (Leeds: Peepal Tree, 2011).

Blanche H. Gelfant, *The Columbia Companion to the Twentieth-Century American Short Story* (New York: Columbia University Press, 2000).

Dana Gioia and R. S. Gwynn, eds, *The Art of the Short Story* (New York and London: Pearson Longman, *c.*2006).

Clare Hanson, ed., *Re-Reading the Short Story* (Basingstoke: Macmillan, 1989).

Clare Hanson, *Short Stories and Short Fictions, 1880–1980* (London: Macmillan, 1985).

Dominic Head, *The Modernist Short Story: A Study in Theory and Practice* (Cambridge: Cambridge University Press, 1992).

Dominic Head, ed., *The Cambridge History of the Short Story* (Cambridge: Cambridge University Press, 1992).

Adrian Hunter, *The Cambridge Introduction to the Short Story in English* (Cambridge: Cambridge University Press, 2007).

Forrest L. Ingram, *Representative Short Story Cycles of the Twentieth Century: Studies in a Literary Genre* (The Hague: Mouton, 1971).

Fredric Jameson, 'Benjamin's Readings', *Diacritics* 22, no. 3/4 (1992), pp. 19–34.

Tim Killick, *British Short Fiction in the Early Nineteenth Century* (Aldershot: Ashgate, 2008).

Maurice A. Lee, ed., *The Multicultural Short Story in the Americas and the Third World* (special issue), *Journal of Modern Literature* 10, no. 1 (1996).

Andrew Levy, *The Culture and Commerce of the American Short Story* (Cambridge: Cambridge University Press, 1993).

David Malcolm, ed., *The British and Irish Short Story Handbook* (Hoboken, NJ: John Wiley & Sons Inc., 2012).

Janet Malcolm, *Reading Chekhov* (New York: Random House, 2001).

Paul March-Russell, *The Short Story: An Introduction* (Edinburgh: Edinburgh University Press, 2009).

Charles E. May, ed., *The New Short Story Theories* (Athens, Oh.: Ohio University Press, 1994).

Lee Clark Mitchell, *More Time: Contemporary Short Stories and Late Style* (Oxford: Oxford University Press, 2019).

Frank Myszor, *The Modern Short Story* (Cambridge: Cambridge University Press, 2000).

Joyce Carol Oates, 'A Land of Shame', *TLS*, 25 Oct. 2013, pp. 21–2.

Frank O'Connor, *The Lonely Voice: A Study of the Short Story* (London: Macmillan, 1963).

Seán Ó Faoláin, *The Short Story* (London: Collins, 1948).

Chris Power, 'A Brief Survey of the Short Story'. *The Guardian*: <https://www.theguardian.com/books/series/abriefsurveyoftheshortstory>.

Ian Reid, *The Short Story* (London: Methuen, 1977).

Ann Shukman, 'The Short Story: Theory, Analysis, Interpretation' in *Essays in Poetics* 2, no. 2 (September 1977), pp. 27–95.

David Staines, ed., *The Cambridge Companion to Alice Munro* (Cambridge: Cambridge University Press, 2016).

Lorin Stein and Sadie Stein, eds, *Object Lessons: The Paris Review Presents the Art of the Short Story* (New York: Picador, 2012).

Thomas E. Swann and Kinya Tsuruta, eds, *Approaches to the Modern Japanese Short Story* (Tokyo: Waseda University Press, 1982).

Index

For the benefit of digital users, indexed terms that span two pages (e.g., 52–53) may, on occasion, appear on only one of those pages.

A

Aiken, Conrad 13
Akutagawa, Ryunosuke 46
  'In a Bamboo Grove' 66–7
Allen, Woody 24
Antrim, Donald 74
Asimov, Isaac 8, 48–9
Atwood, Margaret 25
  Happy Endings 76–8
Austen, Jane 16
Auster, Paul 48–9

B

Babel, Isaac 81–2
Baldwin, James 30, 87
  'Going to Meet the Man' 90–3
Balzac, Honoré de 49–52
Bang, John Kendrick 17
Banville, John 96–7
Barthelme, Donald 22, 74, 80, 103
Baudelaire, Charles 49–51
Beattie, Ann 25
Beckett, Samuel 18, 41–2
Bellem, Robert 6–7
Bellow, Saul 23, 48–9
Bennett, Arnold 11–12
Benson, E. F. 64–5
Borges, Jorge Luis 75
Bowen, Elizabeth 81–2
Boyd, William 94–6
Bradbury, Ray 8, 18
Brande, Dorothea 32–3
Bulwer-Lytton, Robert 2
Burroughs, Edgar Rice 8

C

Cabrera Infante, Guillermo 74
Calvino, Italo 74, 80
Carver, Raymond 94–5
  'Errand' 98–101, 106
catharsis 81, 85–6
causality 73–4
Chandler, Raymond 8, 17, 65–6
character
  agency 19, 87–93, 106
  as determining factor 19, 27–8, 75, 81
  change 108–9

character (*cont.*)
experience determining voice 34–5
morality and 116–17
psychology 95, 103, 113–14, 116–17
self-deception 104, 106
Cheever, John 94–5
'The Country Husband' 109–12
Chekhov, Anton 9–10, 21–2, 36–7, 94–106, 108
'A Doctor's Visit' 97
Conrad, Joseph 10–11
Coover, Robert 22
Cortázar, Julio 74

D

Daly, Carroll John 8
Davis, Lydia 19–20
Ten Stories about Flaubert 77–8
DeLillo, Don 80
Depression, the Great 5–6, 13
Desai, Anita 22
'Diamond Dust' 85–6, 92–3
detective fiction 6–8, 17, 49–50, 64–8, 80
dialect and accent 31–2, 38–40
dialogue 36–8, 41–7
Dickens, Charles 2, 10–11
Dostoevsky, Fyodor 24, 30, 32, 48–51, 94–5
Doyle, Arthur Conan 17, 64–5
Dreiser, Theodore 13

E

economy of detail 25–8, 36–7, 95–6
Eisenberg, Deborah 18
empathy 96–7, 104
ethics of reading 86–7
existentialism 71–2

F

fantastic 39–40
Faulkner, William 12
fiction and reality, relationship of 2–4, 7–8
financial reward 3, 11
Fitzgerald, F. Scott 13
flash fiction *see* micro-fictions
Ford, Richard 24
'Occidentals' 59–62
fragmented speech 44
framing devices 17, 30–1, 103

G

Gallant, Mavis 52–3, 57
'Speck's Idea' 53–5
García Márquez, Gabriel 30–2
Gardam, Jane
'The Tribute' 83–5, 92–3
Gardner, Erle Stanley 7–8
Garner, Helen 30
ghost stories 64–6
Gide, André 55
Glaspel, Susan 7–8
Gogol, Nikolai 94–5
Grey, Zane 8

H

Hadley, Tessa 95
Hammett, Dashiel 8, 17, 64–5
Hardy, Thomas 10–11
Harte, Bret 13
Hawthorne, Nathaniel 4–5, 12–13
Hemingway, Ernest 12, 57
Hempel, Amy 30–1
Henry, O. 2, 9–10, 13
Highsmith, Patricia, *Little Tales of Misogyny* 78–80
Hoffmann, E. T. A. 17
Howard, Robert 17
Howells, William Dean 9–10, 12
Hughes, Langston 13–14

Hugo, Victor 55
Huston, Zora Neale 48–9

I

Inchbald, Elizabeth 2
Iowa Writers' Workshop 94–5
irony 37–9, 75, 81–93, 97–8, 101–2, 104, 106
Irving, Washington 12–13

J

Jackson, Shirley 18
James, Henry 9–10, 22–4, 57, 64–5, 70–1
  'Madame de Mauves' 58–9
James, M. R. 64–5
Jewett, Sarah Orne
  'A White Heron' 108–10
Jhabvala, Ruth Prawer 22
Jones, Edward P. 31–2, 65–6
Joyce, James 21–2, 48–9, 113
  'Eveline' 32–6

K

Kafka, Franz 73
  'A Country Doctor' 73–4
Keret, Etgar 15, 23–4
Kincaid, Jamaica 30
King, Stephen 18
Kipling, Rudyard 10–13, 30–1
Kundera, Milan 86–7
Kurosawa, Akira 66

L

Laclos, Pierre Choderlos de 58
Larbaud, Valéry 55
Larsen, Nella 82–3
Lasdun, James 100–1
Lawrence, D. H. 13, 18, 113
Leavitt, David 95
Leblanc, Maurice 17
Lee, Vernon 17
Leskov, Nikolai 30–1
Li, Yiun 22
limits of genre 77
Lovecraft, H. P. 8

M

McCullers, Carson 12
McGahern, John 24, 87, 92–3
  'Gold Watch' 87–90
Malamud, Bernard 48–9, 64–5
  'The Magic Barrel' 39–41
Mann, Thomas 13, 26–7, 48–9
Mansfield, Katherine 11–12, 26, 28, 57, 96–7, 104
  'Je ne parle pas français' 50–3, 62
Maugham, William Somerset 9–12, 86–7
Maupassant, Guy de 9–10, 50, 60–2, 67, 81–2, 85, 87, 95–6, 101–2
metafiction 75
micro-fictions 76–7
monologue 24, 32, 50–1, 90
Moore, Lorrie 22
  'Two Boys' 42–5
Montand, Yves 55
moral judgement 96–7
Morand, Paul 12
Munro, Alice 30, 67–9, 94–5, 108–9
  'Hateship, Friendship, Courtship, Loveship, Marriage' 27–9
Munro, Hector (Saki) 82–3, 86–7
Munsey, Frank 5–6
mystery stories 66–8; *see also* detective fiction

N

Nabokov, Vladimir 83, 85–7
narration
  first person 17, 23–5, 30–5
  third person 21–3, 32–7, 39–40, 76–7

narration (*cont.*)
reliability 22–4
retrospective 24–7
national traditions 3, 9–15, 30–1, 66, 94–5
novel, comparisons with 1, 4, 11–12, 16, 19, 25–6, 29, 32, 48–9, 77, 108, 113, 116–17

O

Oates, Joyce Carol 14–15
objectivity 96–7, 99
O'Brien, Edna 94–7
'The Love Object' 113–15
O'Connor, Flannery 94–5
O'Connor, Frank 16, 18, 52–3, 81–2, 104
'A Bachelor's Story' 104–6
Ó Faoláin, Seán 81–2
Oppenheim, E. Phillips 17
OULIPO 55–6, 74
Ozick, Cynthia 95

P

Paley, Grace 95
'A Conversation with my Father' 101–3, 106
Paris (city) 49–63
parody 65–6, 112
Payne, William Morton 9–10
Perec, Georges
'The Runaway' 55–7, 60–2
periodical press 1–15, 41–2, 50
plot 102–3
destiny, sense of 85–7
non-linearity 55–6, 67–8, 74, 78
sensationalism 5–8
structure 1–2, 9, 15, 18–19, 27–8, 31–2, 64–80, 107–8
twists 81–7, 92–3
Poe, Edgar Allan 2–3, 8–9, 12–13, 49–50, 64–5
poetic justice 81, 84–5, 92–3
Porter, Katherine Anne 12
postmodernism 74–6, 78–80, 103
Powell, Dawn 12
Pritchett, V. S. 11–12, 30, 106

Q

Queneau, Raymond 74

R

readership
breadth of 4–5, 9
foreign 3, 9–11, 13–15
realism 12, 22, 36–7, 46, 69, 75; *see also* fiction and reality, relationship of
Rhys, Jean 32
Runyon, Damon 37
Russian Formalists 75

S

Saki, *see* Munro, Hector
Sartre, Jean-Paul, 'The Wall' 71–2, 80
Saunders, George, 'Victory Lap' 28, 45–6
Scott, Sir Walter 30–1
serialization 7–10, 13–14
setting
rural 59
urban 48–51, 54, 56–62
Shalamov, Varlaam, 'The Lawyers' Conspiracy' 72–4, 78
Shiel, M. P. 17
Singer, I. B. 48–9, 107–8
Sittenfeld, Curtis 15
Smith, Ali 103
social change 8
social comedy 83–5, 98–9
social commentary 52–3, 57–8, 87, 90–3
Spark, Muriel 41–2, 67, 86–7
status of short story genre 4–6, 8–9

Steinbeck, John 48–9
Stevenson, R. L. 13, 17
Sue, Eugène 49–50
suspense 69–71, 78–80
Suvorin, Aleksei 96
symbolism 42–3, 58–9, 73–4, 88–90, 92–3

T

Taylor, Elizabeth, 'Fly Paper' 68–71
Tolstoy, Leo 16, 22, 32, 67–9
Trevor, William 22, 26–7
Truffaut, François 55
Turgenev, Ivan 22, 30–1, 48–9, 102
typography 19, 43–4

U

Updike, John 14–15, 64–5
'Domestic Life in America' 112

V

viewpoint 22–3
multiplicity 45–6, 99
objectivity and subjectivity of 21–2, 27, 105–6
see also narrative

W

Wallace, Arthur 6–7
Wallace, David Foster 24
Watson, James 12
Wells, H. G. 10–12
Welty, Eudora 25–6, 31–2, 48–9, 67–9, 94–5, 106
Wharton, Edith 9–10, 30–1, 57–8, 60–1, 64–5, 81–2
Williams, Joy 16
Wilson, Angus 13–14
Wolff, Tobias 87
'Hunters in the Snow' 114–17
Wood, James 94–5, 108
Wright, Richard 12

Y

Yates, Richard, 'The Best of Everything' 36–9

ENGLISH LITERATURE

A Very Short Introduction

Jonathan Bate

Sweeping across two millennia and every literary genre, acclaimed scholar and biographer Jonathan Bate provides a dazzling introduction to English Literature. The focus is wide, shifting from the birth of the novel and the brilliance of English comedy to the deep Englishness of landscape poetry and the ethnic diversity of Britain's Nobel literature laureates. It goes on to provide a more in-depth analysis, with close readings from an extraordinary scene in King Lear to a war poem by Carol Ann Duffy, and a series of striking examples of how literary texts change as they are transmitted from writer to reader.

{No reviews}

WRITING AND SCRIPT

A Very Short Introduction

Andrew Robinson

Without writing, there would be no records, no history, no books, and no emails. Writing is an integral and essential part of our lives; but when did it start? Why do we all write differently and how did writing develop into what we use today? All of these questions are answered in this *Very Short Introduction*. Starting with the origins of writing five thousand years ago, with cuneiform and Egyptian hieroglyphs, Andrew Robinson explains how these early forms of writing developed into hundreds of scripts including the Roman alphabet and the Chinese characters.

'User-friendly survey.'

Steven Poole, The Guardian

Bestsellers

A Very Short Introduction

John Sutherland

'I rejoice', said Doctor Johnson, 'to concur with the Common Reader.' For the last century, the tastes and preferences of the common reader have been reflected in the American and British bestseller lists, and this *Very Short Introduction* takes an engaging look through the lists to reveal what we have been reading - and why. John Sutherland shows that bestseller lists monitor one of the strongest pulses in modern literature and are therefore worthy of serious study. Along the way, he lifts the lid on the bestseller industry, examines what makes a book into a bestseller, and asks what separates bestsellers from canonical fiction.

> 'His amiable trawl through the history of popular books is frequently entertaining'
>
> Scott Pack, The Times

www.oup.com/vsi

GERMAN LITERATURE
A Very Short Introduction

Nicholas Boyle

German writers, from Luther and Goethe to Heine, Brecht, and Günter Grass, have had a profound influence on the modern world. This *Very Short Introduction* presents an engrossing tour of the course of German literature from the late Middle Ages to the present, focussing especially on the last 250 years. Emphasizing the economic and religious context of many masterpieces of German literature, it highlights how they can be interpreted as responses to social and political changes within an often violent and tragic history. The result is a new and clear perspective which illuminates the power of German literature and the German intellectual tradition, and its impact on the wider cultural world.

> 'Boyle has a sure touch and an obvious authority . . . this is a balanced and lively introduction to German literature.'
>
> Ben Hutchinson, TLS

www.oup.com/vsi

French Literature

A Very Short Introduction

John D. Lyons

The heritage of literature in the French language is rich, varied, and extensive in time and space; appealing both to its immediate public, readers of French, and also to aglobal audience reached through translations and film adaptations. *French Literature: A Very Short Introduction* introduces this lively literary world by focusing on texts - epics, novels, plays, poems, and screenplays - that concern protagonists whose adventures and conflicts reveal shifts in literary and social practices. From the hero of the medieval *Song of Roland* to the Caribbean heroines of *Tituba, Black Witch of Salem* or the European expatriate in Japan in *Fear and Trembling*, these problematic protagonists allow us to understand what interests writers and readers across the wide world of French.

www.oup.com/vsi